DYING

AN AMISH MAN FAKES HIS DEATH

TO FIND HIS LIFE

Based on the true story of Levi Hochstetler

Compiled from personal interviews and written
by **Sally Pfoutz**

Proper names and identifying details have been changed throughout this work.

Copyright © Sally Pfoutz 2019

Augusta, Wisconsin 1996

Late one August night in small white frame house in a very strict Old Order Amish community that does not have electricity, running water, or telephones, a man starts a bloody trail across the bedroom floor next to the double bed where his young wife sleeps soundly. The blood trail snakes down the narrow staircase through the kitchen out onto the front stoop and onto the gravel drive where it ends in a pool, so that Levi Hochstetler, age 21, will appear to have been taken violently from his bed.

After awhile something wakes up Levi's wife Rosanna. Perhaps it is the putrid smell of blood, or the barking dogs outside. She assumes her husband has gone to the outhouse but even in darkness she can see something on the floor. She sits up in bed, switches on the flashlight and discovers the blood trail leading to the stairs and down. Shocked and horrified, she climbs out of bed and steps cautiously over the splashes of blood, escapes outdoors, and races across the dark yard to the house next door where her in-laws hear her urgent cries for help. After tearing through his son's house to see the blood trail with his own eyes, her father-in-law, Joe, must run across a cornfield in the dead of night to call the police on the neighbors' phone.

When the police arrive, the house and driveway are immediately strung with alien yellow crime tape. Levi's wife, parents, siblings, friends and neighbors are questioned exhaustively. At the break of day, police and bloodhounds search the farm buildings, grounds, and surrounding woods and cornfields. An aerial search ensues.

Levi is missing and presumed dead.

One

Just before dark on that Saturday night, Levi had watched from his kitchen window as the taxi came up the drive and stopped in front of his parents' house. The driver didn't try very hard to avoid the two dogs, Hank and Pete. The dogs rushed and lunged at the tires, barking to beat the band, but the mutts were good at dodging horse hooves and carriage wheels so a motorized vehicle wouldn't be any more dangerous just not as fun, since the van didn't rear up, kicking and snorting. They gave it their best shot though, jumping on the driver's door with their jarring rat-a-tat-tats, not so much behaving as guard dogs as just plain having a good time. That is, until the driver honked the horn long and loud, threw open the door to force them off the car, and sent both dogs reeling back around to the other side where Levi's dad was quick to get out of the car as he shouted commands. "Sit...quiet...get down!"

Levi knew his father's anger was directed at the driver, not the dogs, but he wouldn't dare say anything to the man. The dogs stood by while Levi's father reached in the side door to help his wife step out. Then he leaned in through the front passenger window to pay the driver, while she greeted the dogs with pats all around. Levi's sisters and his brother, Daniel, soon spilled out the front door to help unload.

"Shall we go, too, Levi?" Rosanna inquired.

He shook his head. "No need, Rosanna." And he watched the small group clump together in the grass in order to avoid the van as it backed around awkwardly, and nearly bumped into the big oak tree, before jerking sharply and fairly careening down the gravel drive as if the driver couldn' wait to get away from the Amish. Levi bit his lips to keep from grinning guiltily, for he understood that feeling all too well.

Exactly one week before, with the milking done for the morning, Levi had left Little White Foot, their most docile heifer, confined to the stall. They didn't usually name the cows but Little White Foot's mother had rejected her when she was born, had tried to kill her, in fact, so the ornery cow was led away and shut in the dry lot where she caterwauled something terrible until she fell over dead of a ruptured uterus.

By that time, Edna, being the second oldest girl in the family and not yet able to be so much help with the more womanly pursuits like sewing, was delegated to sit up half the night, taking care of the calf, dripping milk from a baby bottle onto its tongue, teaching it how to suckle, and stroking its tiny crooked white foot until it fell asleep from exhaustion.

Now a hefty 1200 pounds, Little White Foot was still as docile as ever. After breakfast, Levi had stepped into the stall with her and nudged her to make her move over, and then he pinched a chunk of her neck to loosen it up before plunging the needle in and pulling back slowly until the blood reached the 500 cc mark. She was accustomed to being handled, poked and prodded. He was used to giving her shots. It hardly took any time at all. She snorted and shifted on her feet but she didn't try too hard to move away. It was all done in a few minutes. He quickly ducked out of the stall and poured the blood into a jar, screwing the lid on tight before tucking it out of sight in his waistband. He put the cap back on the needle and pocketed it, and then he opened the stall gate and said, "Come on, girl," as he slapped her on the rump to shoo her out into the yard.

Levi watched Little White Foot follow the dirt cattle trail down toward the stream where the rest of the herd was milling around and then he stepped over a pile of manure and left the barn, shutting the door firmly. At twenty-one years-old, he'd spent three-quarters of his life tending the dairy cows, working and driving the horses, he'd even learned how to trim hooves and pull nails on loose shoes. Besides that, farming and carpentry was all he knew.

Levi scanned the farmyard for family members. He looked up toward the two houses, over to the wash shed, the workshop, and the buggy barn. No one was in sight. He walked on up to the house then, using a casual stride, yet having to hold his wrist against the jar of blood in his waistband to keep it from dropping down his pants leg. If anyone saw him they might think he was working on a hernia just like his father, for this was the way his father had maneuvered about with one hand up against his middle protectively, while wincing in pain, although if Levi's face was set in a grimace it was only because he was casting a furtive eye.

He approached the kitchen door quietly, listening for Rosanna. She was an attentive wife and would notice the odd angle of his hand against his waist. She wouldn't just inquire but would rush to his side and take his hand to assess the injury, causing the jar to fall down through his pants leg and roll out onto the kitchen floor and that would be the beginning of the end of his plan.

But the house was empty, so Rosanna must have been out in the garden. There were only the usual summer sounds around him: birds, crickets, squirrels, cats, dogs, chickens, horses, cows, dry thump of his feet on the stoop, and creaking screen door.

In the kitchen he glanced about for a place to hide the jar, saw his denim jacket hanging on the peg by the chimney door and went straight to it. He took it down and placed the jar of blood in the inside pocket, pulled the jacket closed and put it back on the peg with its front to the wall, draped to make the pockets' contents inconspicuous.

Now everything was coming together. That night he'd wait for Rosanna to fall asleep before creeping downstairs to get the jar of blood, race back up, quiet as a ghost, and leave a trail of dripping blood from the bedside, across the floor, down the stairs, through the kitchen to the gravel drive out front where he'd dump the rest. He'd decided on a stabbing and kidnapping for several reasons: the brethren wouldn't blame him for leaving because he'd been taken against his will, presumably injured and abducted. Also for these same reasons, his family would not have to confess his sins before the church and most importantly, if they thought he was dead they wouldn't come after him to browbeat him and force him to return.

He'd come up with the idea of leaving a blood trail that ended with a pool of blood in the drive because he figured that when a person was stabbed and carried through the house there'd be dripping blood, but when he was loaded into the getaway car, there'd be a gush of blood. It was an Amish kid's idea of what a stabbing and kidnapping would look like, and he didn't have much to go on. He actually had nothing to go on, but his own imagination and the image of the animals they butchered for meat.

His only view of the outside world, what they called the English world, was when he worked off the family farm for other Amish, driving his buggy a few miles in one direction, a few miles in the other. He knew bad things happened in the English world, but he'd never heard any newscasts since they had no radios or televisions. Certainly he could read, but growing up, they only read the Bible or non-violent novels like Little House on the Prairie and Nancy Drew. And while the Bible was full of revenge, murder, beatings and kidnappings, there were no real details to go on and it was much too far removed from the present time. So Levi had to make it up, and he'd rarely had so much fun in his life as he did when he planned his escape.

What a week it had been. He was about to bust at the seams. Now he had the cow blood, the cash, and the English clothes, everything he needed to get away. What luck that his mother kept bags of rags, some of them English clothes, up in the attic. On Tuesday when his father and brother were repairing barbed wire along the road and Rosanna and his mother and sisters were at a quilting bee, Levi had gone up in the attic, found the bags, and emptied them out. There was a white button down shirt with lay-down collar and gray dress pants—English clothes! He tried them on. The shirt was fine but the pants were a little short. They'd have to do. They would do. There wasn't a hat, why would there be a hat in a rag bag? But he'd rough up his hair until he could get it shorn. His big bowl cut of thick black hair was worse than a sign telling the world he was Amish.

He rolled the shirt and pants together and placed them in one of the plastic bags, stuffed everything else back in the others, and rushed down from the attic. Outside, feeling the need to hurry now that he had the stolen clothes in his possession, Levi practically ran to the wash shed. Since Monday was wash day and he'd be gone by Saturday, he thought the wash shed was a good place to hide the clothes. He took a metal wash tub down from the wall and brushed the spider webs out of it. It obviously wasn't one anyone used. He put the bag of clothes inside it and hung it back on the wall. Then he left.

Just as he was making his way over toward the barn he heard the buggy coming up the drive with the women. He went into the barn and snatched a harness off the wall, grabbed a rag and began cleaning the leather. When the buggy pulled up Levi set down the rag and harness, greeted everyone and asked how the morning had gone. They were happy, even Rosanna smiled pleasantly as she climbed out and followed the others toward his parents' house.

Levi unhitched the horse, walked her around to cool her off before he gave her a rub down and then turned her loose in the grassy paddock. Rosanna called to him from his mother's kitchen door. "We're putting up beans this afternoon, Levi, would you like me to make you a sandwich first?"

"No thanks, I ate awhile ago." He went back to cleaning the harnesses. It wasn't one of his chores but no one would begrudge him doing it. Sometime after that, he was so lost in thought he couldn't say if it was five minutes or an hour, he happened to look up just as his mother was leaving the wash shed carrying that very same seldom-used gray metal wash tub in which he'd hidden the plastic bag of English clothes. He felt his face blanch and his heart began a drumbeat inside his chest.

He watched her closely from under his eyelashes, his hands automatically continuing the harness cleaning. He couldn't tell from her posture what she might be thinking. She wasn't walking particularly fast, as she might if she were going to tell them what she'd found, or if something disturbed her. He wasn't close enough to see her face, to read her expression. He knew when she was tired, he could tell when she was angry, and she had a wonderful laugh that filled him with happiness. But her face was turned away from him. Had she seen the clothes? Had she wondered what in the world they were doing inside the washtub?

He finished the entire wall of harnesses, swept up, and left the barn, taking the long way around to the wash shed. Inside he saw the plastic bag lying on the floor with the clothes still inside it. For some reason his mother had taken the wash tub down from the wall and if she was surprised to see the bag of clothes inside it, she hadn't seemed to be curious enough to do any more than to drop the bag on the floor. He snatched up the bag, stuffed it under his shirt and went back out, trying not to appear suspicious in case someone was looking. He decided there and then that if anyone asked what he was doing in the wash shed, he'd say he wanted to ask his mother a question. What question?

Luckily he made it to the workshop before he was forced to think of something for when was the last time he'd sought his mother out to ask her anything other than how are you and other pleasantries? It had been years. In the workshop, with trembling hands and a recovering heart, he left the bag of clothes behind a pile of scrap wood. It wasn't such an unusual place to leave a bag of rags.

So now he was all set. He had the jar of cow blood, English clothes to change into for the getaway, and two hundred dollars in cash he had squirreled away a few dollars at a time from his outside earnings. He knew where there was a car he could take—and though he had never driven a car, he had watched drivers move the lever to the D and step on the long pedal to make it go and the short pedal to stop.

Saturday finally arrived. As always, he got up at 4:30 in the morning and went out to milk the cows, and he was elated, because it would be the last time, the last stinking time. Tomorrow when the sun came up, he'd be gone. But as he pulled the collar over number 4's head, and nudged the bucket under her with one boot, while repositioning the stool with his other, he heard a car go by outside.

He let go of the cow, shoved her head aside and squeezed past. He peered out the gaps in the barn wall. A van sat in front of his parents' house. They had hired a taxi. Levi fell back against the wall and let out a long sigh of disappointment. The cows started rumbling in the open box stall, banging against the wood sides and mooing as each one pushed against the one in front to move out of the way. That kicked up a stench of cow piss and dung so rank he hid his nose and mouth in the crook of his arm.

He'd forgotten—his parents were going to his cousin's wedding in Michigan. It all came to him like a sudden recollection and he slapped his hand against the wood beam in dismay. They'd be gone an entire week, and that meant there was no way he could leave. He wouldn't do that to Rosanna and his sisters or his little brother Daniel, stick them with the milking and farming, and other chores. A horse could get injured or a cow, hurt so badly that it would have to be shot, and that wasn't something Daniel could do and certainly not any of the women. Levi's older brother Samuel hadn't been back to help out since he moved off the place so there was no point in counting on him. Levi would have to wait until his parents returned.

Slowly, he went back to finish the milking. The cows had scattered when they had the chance and were now all clustered in and around the hay. He brought them back one by one, collared them and milked, said hello to Daniel who was there to fill the milk cans while Levi fed the cows and released them, shoveled out the stalls, and swept up. By that time the van was gone and Daniel had set the milk cans out, ready for pick up.

His parents were gone, and Levi was disconsolate. It wasn't as if he'd lost his chance, he told himself. He could go through with his plan the next Saturday night, as soon as his parents were home again. But what if he lost his nerve? Could he go through the motions for seven days knowing all along what lay ahead? Levi had always been restless, his entire life, and once he had committed to leave it would take immense resolve to tuck it all back inside.

Something could happen between now and then that would force him to stay. What if his parents died in a wreck? What if Rosanna got pregnant? It could even be the thing he dreaded, the thing he knew was coming. His grandfather could suddenly decide that the community needed another minister and he'd be chosen, he knew. He had seen it in the way they considered him with their stern eyes. His grandfather was a bishop, his father was a minister, his older brother Samuel had shown himself to be unworthy, while Levi had done everything right, outwardly he was a good Amish man, even if inwardly he was not. If he didn't go now he'd get sucked in and cemented in place and his life would be over.

No, it had to be now; this month, this summer. Ever since Samuel moved out Levi had felt responsibility bearing down on him. It was time. He would go as soon as his parents were home again. It complicated things so much that he was married. Two years! It was hard to believe. Back then, and it seemed so long ago, he had done what his buddies were all doing, courting, and then marrying. Rosanna was the only girl he had ever dated, and he did not regret her presence in his life, but it was very difficult, nearly impossible to look her in the eyes now. He had to hide his plans from the very person who knew him best.

 Levi went up to the house and in through the kitchen door. Rosanna approached him earnestly, sweetly and handed him a dishtowel so he could wash up. She couldn't conceal her pleasure at having his parents gone. Living at their farm, working side-by-side with his mother and his sisters had been difficult for her. Rosanna was so shy; it was hard for her to feel at ease around them. They never spoke against her, but she didn't think that they liked her very much and Levi suspected that it might be true.

 Rosanna seemed aloof because she was such an introvert and that tended to make people suspicious, especially women. But he knew it was her seeming aloofness that had made their courtship work. Levi was gregarious. He was outspoken and confident and he did what needed to be done. Rosanna held back. She was watchful and private. She didn't mind that Levi got all the attention, and in fact, she preferred it. But there were so many hours in the day when he was out working and she was at home with his mother and sisters and it hurt that the other women didn't seem to accept her. "I have a mother," she'd exclaim, "I'm not looking for another mother or even sisters. I just want to feel a part of your family, Levi." Rosanna missed her own family so much. She was homesick.

 "They're protective of me," he'd tell her when she worried out loud. "I'm the favorite son now that Samuel is gone." And when he'd hear himself put into words exactly that which felt like a noose around his neck, he'd feel all the more committed to his plan. He was only sorry he couldn't let her know that he was going to leave;

he almost wished he could take her with him but he didn't think she'd go, they had never spoken about it but he knew Rosanna. She wouldn't want to hurt her parents. And how could he ask her to leave, knowing she would never see her family again? It was too cruel. So he kept it to himself and tried not to brood.

Levi and Rosanna were definitely opposites, where she hung back and waited for life to fall into her lap, he was tireless, always reaching, striving, and trying new things. Levi wanted to be the best at whatever he did. He wanted to come in first, and often he did, because Samuel only did enough to get by. When they were teenagers working beside their father building craft items for The Woodshed, an "Amish-made" store in Augusta, their father told them that any money they made on their own time they could keep for themselves. Levi was out at the workshop almost every night, hammering and sawing, saving the money—his money, while Samuel had been off hanging around with his buddies, smoking cigarettes, even trying alcohol from time to time.

"Your parents have left for Michigan. Did you remember, Levi?"

He glanced up in confusion. Only the Lord knew what she'd seen on his face when he walked through the doorway. How long had he been standing there doing nothing? He had no idea. He placed his glasses on the window ledge, leaned over the bucket, and splashed his face over and over, snatched up a towel as he straightened up, still with his back to her, and mopped at his beard and briskly rubbed his forehead and the sides of his face until his skin was dry. He didn't want to turn around. He was afraid of what she'd see in his eyes, anger and despair.

"Levi?"

"I remember, Rosanna," he replied, still stunned to have all his careful planning thwarted by his parents' trip to Michigan.

Rosanna set his breakfast on the table and eyed him curiously. "Is it the chores?" she asked a little too brightly. "I'll help more now that Samuel is gone."

Levi was furious at himself. He eyed his jacket that hung on the farthest peg—if he squinted he imagined he could make out the jar of cow blood in one pocket and the folded money in the other. It was already steaming hot outside though the sun had been up barely half an hour and that's why his jacket was a safe hiding place--unless Rosanna had a sudden urge to wash it, but that was unlikely given all the canning that took place in summer. She was far too busy with the garden to go around looking for additional items to add to the laundry.

Everything he'd done in preparation seemed to mock him. Even the bag of clothes nestled amongst the pile of scrap wood in the workshop, he could picture the little plastic bag in his mind's eye harboring the ill-fitting English clothes. So he'd been all set to go and now he'd have to postpone it for an entire week. The important thing was that no one could suspect that he planned to leave at all; no one.

Levi went back to washing up. Again, he splashed water on his face, over and over, as if he needed to wake up. Rosanna held the towel for him. She retrieved his glasses and cleaned them on her apron before carefully setting them on his face, tucking the wires behind his ears. Her eyes were gentle like a mother's. "I can milk a cow, Levi," she reminded him. "I can get up with you and help. I want to." Her head was tilted sweetly as she smiled up at him.

Levi kissed her on the cheek, and then covered his embarrassment by going to the window and looking out. He never kissed her like that, impulsively. He had to be careful. She put her hand on his shoulder and squeezed. He rested his hand on top of hers as if he were confirming that he had been concerned about doing the chores alone, when in fact he enjoyed being by himself and not under his father's watchful critical eye. He sat down at the table and began to eat the hot cereal; hot cereal in the middle of July. Did everything always have to be exactly the same? He wondered what the English ate on hot summer mornings. Ice cream, maybe? Cold watermelon?

Rosanna set a plate of biscuits and gravy next to the bowl of cereal and sat down across from him with her chin in her hands. She was so pretty with her dark frizzy hair and deep set brown eyes but her looks weren't enough to keep him there. He glanced up and smiled his thanks, then continued eating without talking, knowing that there was something about his young wife that made him want to carp about his family. She encouraged it. He had definitely complained to her probably a great deal more than he should have that he really missed Samuel's help on the farm. But the fact was he just plain missed working alongside his brother. For heaven's sake he'd being doing it since he was six.

Their father was a good strong worker but ever since he became a minister when Levi was barely seven, he had hardened, become even stricter. He was always tense and judging, correcting, far too serious, as if he had the weight of the world on his shoulders, and in a sense he did. Their world was the Amish settlement in which they lived and the church elders like his father made all the decisions regarding financial matters, such as, which families needed help with medical bills and other expenses.

The elders also set the rules of the community and while the entire congregation heard individuals' confessions, it was the elders who decided upon punishment. What was worse for Levi and the other sons of elders, (and he suspected for their fathers, too), was that young people were required to confess all indiscretions, including those most embarrassing acts they'd been unable to resist committing, by themselves, in private. It was a sin to touch oneself for pleasure, after all, and one confessed one's sins in order to be forgiven and hearing these confessions every other week was just more than Levi could bear, yet another reason why he was simply fed up with being Amish.

"Levi?"

Rosanna got up and cleared the table, having to make three trips because she was tiny. Her little hands and thin arms could never manage the balancing act he was accustomed to—his mother and sisters would have two plates in each hand with cups stacked on top and dishes resting on their wrists and arms all the way up to their elbows. Rosanna was careful with the dishes as if they were priceless but he knew it was difficult for her to set them down in the sink. Why, she even needed to stand on a stool to dip water from the bucket.

He'd made her that stool when they were courting. He had carved it into the shape of a butterfly and painted it dark blue. She'd acted like it was a prize and she had been so pleased, that for a wedding present he'd made her a rocking chair of carefully quarter sawn oak. It had a curved back and wide arms. She had been thrilled.

Rosanna was only four feet eight inches with arms and legs as thin as pretzels. She still used little girl patterns to make her clothes. Sometimes it made him smile and call her Little Bit but not that day. "We'll be okay for the week. I'll help you," she said again.

He shook it off inwardly, all of it, his irritation at her for being so innocent, for wanting to help with the heavy chores, his anger at himself for setting up his escape on the very Saturday that his parents were going away, his resentment of his parents for being Amish, for bringing him into the Amish world, for choosing that week to go to Michigan.

"I know, Rosanna."

Though he wouldn't send her out to milk the cows or lead the horses for any amount of money in the world. She was simply too small. She'd get hurt and then it would be his duty to take care of her for the rest of their lives. He'd never be able to leave the Amish.

He crossed the room, took his straw hat from the peg and went out onto the front stoop where he looked once more at his parents' house. He should thank the Lord that his sister Edna was old enough to take care of the others or he and Rosanna would have to sleep over there. He raised his eyebrows in sheer relief at that and muttered to himself as he went to the workshop to build shelves.

It shouldn't have been a surprise to him that his parents were going away. He'd heard about his cousin's wedding months before, and hiring a taxi to go all the way to Michigan was an expensive endeavor, which they had to plan far in advance. His mother had been over just the day before to have Rosanna pin up the new dress she'd made for the wedding—dark blue as always, but not the everyday broadcloth, something a little dressier that had a swirling skirt and a bit of a shine to it. The dress was new, that was the main thing. Most of his mother's clothes were decades old, the material dusty-looking, wrinkled and faded, just as his mother herself had so often appeared to him there in the background with her sad face pining and untended like a mare that lost a foal. In fact he'd seen that look on her face from the time he was seven, when his little brother died.

Yes, he was certain he'd been told about their trip, but he simply had not paid attention as preoccupied as he had been with making his own plans. Besides, his parents always went away in summer after the second hay cutting. What was the matter with him that he'd not thought of it? It was only one more week; he'd been Amish for twenty-one years; he could endure it for seven more days and nights.

And now they were back. He watched his family troop inside and the screened door announced each one's arrival with a hardy slap against the wood frame. Still Levi watched as the dogs finished sniffing the pathways and trotted off to bother something else over on the other side of the barn. The white house across the way—the house he grew up in—was nearly identical to the one he and Rosanna lived in now. Each was tidy and modest, and between them they shared a patch of grass, a big oak tree, a purple flowered lilac bush, a white Rose of Sharon, and a clothesline.

Their house, his and Rosanna's, had originally been built for Levi's oldest sister and her husband, but they had moved shortly before Levi married Rosanna and so it became theirs. Rosanna pretended to like it, for it was spacious and clean and there was lots of natural light, but he knew she would prefer that they, also, could get their own place off his parents' farm. If they had been able to live on their own, he might not have been so intent upon leaving. He might have stayed on, but that certainly wasn't going to happen now. He tried not to look too far into the future but if Edna were to marry then the house would be hers, for Rosanna would not want to stay there by herself. Perhaps she'd move back home with her parents after he disappeared.

The sun set quickly in their Wisconsin valley, blue, hazy pink, yellow at the horizon and it was down. Then the two giant oaks on either side of the gravel drive became hulking shadows until the sliver of moon rose. When his eyes adjusted to the night sky Levi could see angular pine trees silhouetted over the fence line and below that green marble deer eyes dotting the landscape like tiny stars. Closer by the house, curly-topped orchard trees formed an orderly squad behind the woodshop. Cows mooed, crickets and cicadas called to each other, tree frogs chirped, and people in the house next door—his family— unpacked in the kitchen, and prepared for slumber upstairs.

They didn't have electricity, they never had. They were Amish of the oldest order, and in two short hours, he would be no longer. What were the things he wanted to do when he was free? Drive a truck. Take a hot shower. Have a job and for once in his life make his own income. Go where he wanted, when he wanted, with whomever he pleased. He wanted to be responsible for himself alone and not an entire community. He would finally for the first time in his life be completely on his own, free to think his own thoughts, to make decisions for himself alone, a simple need he imagined most English men had—and English women, too, he suspected. He wondered how his marriage would have fared if he and Rosanna had lived somewhere else and he felt bad that he hadn't been able to provide her with their own place. Too late to concern himself with that now but maybe he wouldn't have decided to leave the Amish if he and Rosanna had been on their own and not right under his parents' noses.

    Levi shifted his gaze to block the glare of lantern light against his eyeglasses, and he watched his mother in her kitchen pulling items from plastic grocery bags, jars and cans, and passing them on to his sister to put away. His father went out to check on the animals, not because he had any reason to, except that he had been gone a week and was glad to be back doing the things he always did.

    Levi watched his mother and sister bustle about the kitchen across the way, his mother and Edna now silhouettes in lantern light and he squinted toward the barn. He could just make out the flickering beam of a flashlight as his father moved from the cow enclosure to the horse stalls. The horses snorted and the cows mooed. There were several loud thumps as hooves collided with barn walls, or weird wails of protest when a dominant animal head-butted, kicked or bared his big teeth and sunk them into the hide of a weaker member of the herd.

    They had eight horses, two Standardbreds, one for his buggy and one for his father's, plus six drafts to do the farming. They preferred Percherons. He liked the horses better than the cows even though they were just transportation, while the cows produced milk and therefore gave his family a livelihood. Still he preferred the horses mainly because he understood them. Horses were fairly consistent and predictable and cows were the opposite.

    If a horse became frightened his instinct was to run away. A cow might also run away but he could just as easily turn on you, charge, and try to stick you with his horns or trample you. His father complained if Levi fussed over the horses in the least or if he didn't discipline them appropriately. But his father thought hitting a horse over the head with a two-by-four was proper discipline for running away with the carriage, even though the horse almost got them killed when a deer leapt across her path and spooked her. It would have been Levi's inclination to catch the horse and calm her down, not beat her. But this was his father's way and he didn't confine this practice to the animals, either. When he was younger, Levi had been hit with a two by four when he disobeyed. It was the Amish way and he didn't even think about begrudging his father, he certainly loved and honored him, he simply did not want to live that way any longer and that meant leaving.

Besides the horses, they had about a dozen cows that they milked and the milk was made into cheese and sold at the Dairy Maid Co-op. There was always an ornery bull to produce calves, a rooster and a henhouse full of chickens, two or three dogs, and a lot of cats. The barnyard was full.

His father came out of the barn, slid the door shut, and went up to his house, not even glancing over to where Levi stood at the window some thirty feet away. As far as his parents knew, it was just an ordinary Saturday night and they'd talk in the morning before church. Levi watched the windows of the house he grew up in from the house next door knowing that he would go to bed that night as if it were any other night and wake up free. He knew he had to make it seem like everything was normal. Rosanna couldn't suspect a thing or she'd lie awake. She had to be sound asleep before he could set the scene, spill the blood trail, grab the bag of clothes and run.

He heard Rosanna go upstairs, undress, unpin her cap, hang it on the bedpost, and take down her hair. It wasn't that he could actually hear her unbutton and unpin, he just knew that every single night it was the same. And yet, he couldn't stop looking out the window. Was he trying to memorize the scenery? Done! He'd never lived anywhere else that he could remember. They had left Missouri when he was four and although he couldn't picture his Grandpa Levi's house, he still had the wagon his grandpa had made for him and he wished he could bring it with him when he left. Why he knew exactly where it sat, next to the pump house, wheels oiled and ready for a day's worth of hauling.

Levi smiled at the memory of his grandfather proudly presenting him with the wagon. He would never forget, never. Still, he was reluctant to leave the window. Was he trying to lure himself into staying? Summer smelled sweet on the farm, waves of corn, five feet tall and growing, soft breeze from the nearby creek, silt and brine, pines rustling, oaks crackling, the sour pinch of cow manure and piss, great puddles of it where it hadn't drained yet, brackish even in the dead of winter and a true steaming stench in summer. It was all he had ever known.

He ducked his head so he could see the blue-black sky. Tonight was better than the Saturday before. Tonight it was dark; practically moonless. That would make it easier for everyone to fall asleep, for him to go, to creep about dripping his blood trail, to steal away through the neighbor's field, into the woods, and out onto the road to town, past the market, to the abandoned house he'd seen, the one with the car out front, the car he'd take to get away, to make his escape. Under cover of the black night, there shouldn't be many people on the road he hoped there wouldn't be anybody to notice his leaving.

Rosanna lay down upstairs, the creaking bed was a dead giveaway. Levi took one last look around, before taking off his glasses and setting them on the kitchen table as he always had. He must do everything the same. It would be difficult to go without his glasses but he had no choice. Kidnappers wouldn't pause to grab their victim's glasses, he knew that much. Besides, he had lived with poor eyesight most of his life; he'd only gotten the eyeglasses a few years before. He was strong and able, he had a stubborn-streak a mile wide, and he'd manage without his glasses as he'd always managed, but he wouldn't like it. As soon as he got a job, he'd buy himself new ones, new glasses and a truck. He'd always wanted to drive a truck.

That decision enabled him to go to bed at last and begin his carefully laid out plans. He climbed the stairs in his same tired way to get into bed beside Rosanna. She knew him as well as anyone, but he didn't think she had even a smidgeon of an idea about what he planned to do. Later, she would be astonished if she ever discovered the truth. She would be afraid and furious and heartbroken and she would never forgive him. He was sorry about that, it worried him a lot more than all the promises of hellfire and damnation if he ever left the Amish.

Levi was a man of strong character, he didn't want to hurt his wife; he didn't want to leave her. He could only imagine how awful she'd feel to be the one whose husband walked out, and so that was another reason why he had to make it look as if he had been kidnapped and stabbed. He had to make it look as though he had been taken against his will, how could she blame him for that?

If they thought he was dead, they would pray for him and mourn him. But he couldn't make it look like a suicide because that was a sin and he was not a sinner. His parents wouldn't be able to abide that, nor he. Levi wasn't giving up his belief in God, he still knew right from wrong he simply did not want to live the Amish life anymore. He would always be Amish. For the rest of his life he'd be Amish. He just would not live the Amish life. And that meant doing everything within his power to minimize the effect his sins would cast upon his family.

Levi undressed and climbed into bed as quietly as he could listening for Rosanna's steady breathing. He needed her to fall into a deep sleep, but what if she had a feeling? Rosanna was the kind of woman who had a feeling often and she was usually accurate. She couldn't know what he was about to do, or it would be impossible, he'd never get away.

She rolled over and kissed him, extending her soft arm across his chest, letting her fingers glide over him, back and forth, and then up and down, over and over. He tried not to hold his breath but it was his natural reaction to her touch. Now that he knew he was going to leave her, he felt it would be false to respond, to put his arms around her and pull her close. At night she was sweet and tentative, yet sometimes bold in her desires. He had liked that. Her nightly ritual of taking off her covering and hanging it over the bedpost, then unpinning her hair. When she'd loosen the braided bun and brush it with her fingers, it was a delight to watch. At first she only did it when the sky was pitch black, as it was that night, but after they'd been married awhile, she had taken to doing it every night, away from the window, of course, but even in early evening light, for his eyes only.
    Just lately she had taken to removing her clothing in front of him—with her back to him, but in full sight. She'd unpin her cape, fold it and place it beside her on the bed. Undo the hooks that held her dress together and let it fall from her shoulders. Each cotton garment was unhooked or unbuttoned carefully and removed neatly until she wore nothing. She wouldn't turn to him until they were under the covers, knowing that this increased his desire a great deal.
    Marriage had changed Rosanna considerably. That she would sit before him with nothing on had come as a big surprise. When they courted, Rosanna had seemed more than shy, reluctant even, but after they married she had taken to reaching for him in bed. He knew it was because she wanted to have a baby and initially he had been startled by her forwardness, but he had grown to expect it, her hands pressing him all over, as she watched him in the darkness, her gaze as sharp and sophisticated as a cat's. During the day her eyes were usually downcast, often sad, though he didn't think she knew it. She had large brown eyes that seemed to focus right on the core of him, and a narrow face. Her touch was kind but also insistent.

She must have been upstairs waiting and waiting, he realized, for it wasn't until he heard her get into bed that he climbed the stairs and he admonished himself for standing at the window for so long. He was supposed to do everything the same and already he'd made a major mistake. She would remember, once he was gone, that on this night, his last night, he had not come to bed until he thought she was asleep.

As if thinking the very same thought, Rosanna stopped stroking him. She sighed and turned over with her back to him, knees bent, arms crossed protectively over her breasts, hands together in prayer; it was her sleeping pose.

Levi lay beside Rosanna and he sweated. Rivulets of nervous perspiration trickled through his hair and down the sides of his neck. His beard was actually damp. One thing that excited him as he lay there, besides getting his driver's license, which was about the first thing he'd do the minute he could, was cutting his hair and shaving his beard. When an Amish man is married he grows a beard and Levi didn't particularly like the itchy hot constant feel of his long black beard and he definitely was sick and tired of the floppy bushy haircut.

Rosanna was finally asleep. He put his hand on her arm to be sure. She didn't move. Her breathing was deep, calm. He kept his hand there to the count of ten, no, twenty. Then he reached for his clothes on the floor, got up carefully and dressed. He glanced at the bed again and again to make sure she wasn't watching. He hoped she was asleep. It wasn't as if he had never gotten up in the night to go to the outhouse. Even if she heard him she wouldn't think anything of it.

He plucked his boots up off the floor and tiptoed downstairs, left them by the table, hesitated for an instant then reached for his glasses, he had to have his glasses he had to be able to see. He went over to his jacket to retrieve the jar of blood, pocketed the cash, then he crept back up to the bedside and stood there for the longest moment testing Rosanna. If she was still awake she would have to ask him, What is it, Levi? Even if her feelings were hurt by his disinterest, he knew her, she wouldn't be able to pretend sleep if he was standing by the bed staring at her.

He carefully unscrewed the cap and started to leave the room, tilting the jar slightly, letting the blood drip along the floor from the bed to the stairs and down into the kitchen and across the floor to the door. Then he went back to the table and stepped into his boots, opened the door carefully, lifting up, to minimize the creaking, closed it silently, and hurried outside, dripping the blood. Out front, he poured the rest of the blood into a pool on the gravel drive and ran over to the woodshop where he'd stored the bag of clothes, opened the door, snatched the bag from behind the pile of scrap wood, then back outside, shutting the door firmly and quietly, and took one last look to see if anyone was about. He willed the dogs not to notice, hoping they were way off somewhere or so sound asleep on his parents' back stoop they wouldn't come bounding and barking to his side.

Then he was off. Levi simply tore through the neighbor's cornfield, zig-zagging down the rows so as not to cut himself on their razor-like leaves. He stopped midway to throw the blood smeared jar in a high arc over the corn. In the woods he kicked off his boots, yanked off his shirt and pants, struggled into the English clothes, snatched the folded bills from one pocket and crammed them into another, looked at the dark sky, figuring about fifteen minutes had passed since he left. He leaned down and tied his boots securely, even double knotting them, not wanting to get tripped up. He looked to the sky but stars weren't out yet.

Since they didn't have electricity at his house they tended to go to bed at nine or ten. It was two miles into town and he didn't pass a living soul. He figured it was about eleven, eleven-thirty when he got to the gas station. At the market, he bought a Mountain Dew and a Snickers bar. He had slicked back his hair as best he could but with his long beard even if he had hidden his hair under a hat it would be pretty obvious he was Amish.

He hesitated in the aisle with his wares, afraid the man would comment on his appearance, but the man behind the counter didn't even look at him when he paid for his soda and candy bar. He could have been wearing a clown costume and that man wouldn't have cared! Still he got out of there before he dared to open the Mountain Dew and take a drink, then another and another, guzzling the soda down as if he were dying of thirst, and maybe he was. He had never drunk anything that bubbled the way the soda did, and was pleasantly surprised and terrified that someone would hear the resounding belch that exploded out of his mouth, but there was no one around to notice.

Levi strode briskly down the side of the road and cast the empty bottle into the woods. He tried to ignore the deep ache in his broken leg. He still thought of it that way, as broken for that was the way it felt, the pain expanding, throbbing, shooting pellets of agony up and down from his hip to his knee. He thought he could actually feel that plate in there with the seven screws attached to his thighbone, rubbing it raw. He was supposed to have had it removed after a year, but they didn't have the money for that. He stopped and ran his hand over his thigh and knee, once, trying to warm it up and diminish the ache.

Then he set off again, limping slightly. By this time in his life, he had worked for other Amish outside of the family farm. He had driven his horse and buggy about and he had noticed an English house another two or two and a half miles away. The house was empty. It was obvious. The yard was overgrown and there was a car out front. He was going to walk there and take the car and drive somewhere, he didn't know where, just drive away. He didn't even think about whether the keys would be in the car; he just assumed they would be, or how he was even going to operate the thing, he would figure it out.

Then he was going to have to hide out, because stealing a car was bad. If he got caught, he'd go to jail.

He trudged along, the limp becoming more and more pronounced. Even his good leg was sore and he began to lose hope that he'd find the car. Had he somehow missed it in the dark night? The bugs were horrible, he was being eaten alive but he didn't care about that, he just needed to get there, to find that car. He was walking very fast, he couldn't help it. He was excited, not afraid, and still there were no passersby.

Suddenly he was struck with the most severe stabbing pain in his leg that he fell down right there by the side of the road, clutching his knee to his chest and rolling back and forth in agony. After the pain subsided, he sat up and caught his breath and that was when he saw the car up ahead. He was eye level with the abandoned house, and the car was still there. He got up gingerly and practically hopped on one foot to keep the weight off his leg, he imagined the metal plate in there chafing against the bone and he added that to his list of things he would do when he had a job. He'd go have the screws removed even though the thought of going back into the hospital turned his stomach and caused the ache to sear a path right through his skull.

Levi stumbled through waist-high weeds toward the car. From the road it had seemed to be brown, but when he got close he could see it was red. Not only was it red but it didn't have any tires. It was a red junk car up on blocks, a fact he hadn't been able to see from the road because of all the weeds. He looked back at the road as if to mock himself of all those times he'd driven by in the buggy feeling so satisfied that his getaway car was still there.

Levi pushed the driver's door handle to open the door but it was stuck. The window behind it was partway open though so he reached in and clasped the top to try and pull it out cleanly but it snapped in two. He carefully extracted the top jagged piece and threw it behind him, then the other half, and he crawled in through the open window and slumped down in the backseat. If he had been the crying sort he'd have been bawling like a baby right about then, but he was stoic, he was practical.

He slept in the car that night, cramped and hurting.

Two
"Levi's Gone!"

Rosanna opened her eyes and felt the empty bed beside her. Levi must have gone to the outhouse. She turned on her side, reached for his pillow and fluffed it for him. Then she tucked her hands under her head and tried to fall back asleep. She said a prayer, she thought about the next morning which was Other Sunday meaning that Levi's parents would be gone for most of the day—his father to conduct church services on the other side of the community, his mother going along as she always did. Rosanna had a lot of canning to do, and Levi always had farm chores or woodworking, but maybe they could go off together just the two of them on a buggy ride and a picnic. She could fry some chicken, make potato salad, and a batch of his favorite snicker-doodles. That made her smile. They hadn't had a private picnic since their courting days.

    She'd ask him when he came back from the outhouse. He had been so pleased when she put together a picnic basket back when they were courting, a picnic might be just the thing to bring him out of his funk.

    Sometimes Rosanna felt amazed at how her life had turned out--married now, sleeping beside Levi. It was all right and good and to be expected, but when she was alone, she had a hard time accepting it because even after two years of marriage, she didn't feel as if she really knew her husband.

    She had been so innocent up until they married, in spite of everything she been told about being a wife; hearing about it was quite a different experience from being there alone with a man, knowing what was expected. Their first argument as husband and wife had happened on their wedding night—even though hardly any words were exchanged.

When Levi asked her to undress, she had begun to do so, clumsily untying her apron and removing it, folding it into a bundle and holding it to her chest while he watched from the bed. "Would you like me to help you undo the buttons on your dress?" he asked her and she froze.

She had been so startled by his question that she just stood there clutching the apron. She felt the little ball of handmade soap her aunt had tucked into the apron pocket and she quickly took it out and placed it on the floor beside her pillow. You'll want this for after, her aunt had whispered. And while Rosanna understood what after meant she didn't know the why. Am I supposed to bathe with it? She'd asked, and her aunt shook her head, no. Just keep it beside your pillow. You'll be able to fall asleep afterwards as you should. It's lavender. Restful.

She placed the folded apron on the bedside table that had been a gift from her grandfather. She stared through her tears at her wedding dress, a dark blue button-up she had made mostly by herself. Her stitches weren't as tight as they could be, though, so her mother had ripped out part of the bodice and re-done it for her. It was pretty. Certainly the nicest dress she had ever worn.

Rosanna turned away from Levi slightly and unbuttoned the dress. Then she remembered her head was still covered and she unpinned her prayer cap, removed it, and placed it on the table. She nervously smoothed down her hair. Her dress was open in the back revealing a white cotton slip and bra and underpants under that. Oh, how she wanted to keep those on. Their eyes met for an instant. Rosanna knew what he was thinking. Levi was intent, he was serious, he had waited a long time for this.

Up until that point Levi had kissed her extensively, their lips locked for hours as they sat together in the courtship rocker at her parents' house. She would sit on his lap turned sideways with her arms around his neck and shoulders in the courting tradition, and he would wrap his arms around her waist. After they decided to marry, he started caressing her on top of her clothes and she had liked that—there—in her parents' house. This was different. She was in his house now—their house— and his parents were right next door.

Levi reached for her and took the dress in his fingers. She raised her arms while he lifted it over her head and hung it on a peg. Then he put his hands on her waist and pulled her to him, lifting her up and squeezing tightly so their chests were pressed together. After awhile he set her down and continued kissing her, touching her bare arms, her underarms, reaching in under the edge of her bra at first just with his fingers, and then with his whole hand. He cupped her breast and she had never felt anything like it, his fingers on her skin. It was heavenly and yet frightening at the same time. Her straps fell down over her shoulders and he gently undid the hooks in back and helped her to step out of her underclothes. She was on the edge of fear, glad for once in her life on this moonless night, that they lived in the dark. What would she have done if he had shined the flashlight on her? Thank goodness he did not.

Levi took off his clothes in a split second and tried to pull her onto the bed but she was frozen in place seeing him like that with his eyes on her. She knew it was not a sin but it felt wrong and she flung herself away from him and wrapped her arms across her chest, even as she recalled her cousin's advice (or warning): On your wedding night you mustn't think too much about it, you just let him guide you. That is what you are meant to do.

"Rosanna," Levi said harshly but his hands were gentle as he pried her fingers from her shoulders and held them in his hot hands protectively before placing them on his chest. The hair there was very soft, surprising her, and she squeezed her eyes shut and blocked out who she was and what she was doing. Soon they were lying in each other's arms on the bed and she felt warm, intense, unbelievable good feelings like the urgent thrill when he put his mouth on her breast, the astonishing surge of power when his hand slid down her stomach and clutched her between her legs.

It's natural, it's natural, she told herself again and again, like a promise, like the words to a hymn. It's natural to explain how her legs knew to open and her hips rose up. It's natural, to drown out the sounds, the squishing, the panting, the grunts, and her own sudden gasp of pain, intense horrible pain as he thrashed against her into the heart of her. Up and down, up and down, and she couldn't see his face and hoped he didn't see hers flooded with tears as she felt the skin inside her being ripped and torn and rubbed completely raw.

When it was over he fell back on his pillow and in moments he was snoring softly. Rosanna was astonished to realize Levi was asleep while she lay there shivering in the strange bed, in the dark room, on her wedding night. She got up and felt the gush of hot liquid trickle out from between her legs. She put on her underpants and her slip, reached for the soap on the floor and got back in bed. She was a wife now. So this is what the women had to endure.

It had only been a half hour, she guessed, since Levi had led the way upstairs, hung her clothes on the pegs to the right of the bed. Their new double bed her father had made had been placed in the center of the room, to the right of the window. The rocker Levi had made for her sat across the room near the stairs. On the floor next to the bed there was a large flashlight, and her small blue and black braided rug, a gift from her mother.

"This side is mine," Levi said as he limped over to the window and looked out. She could tell his leg hurt and she wished he hadn't insisted on getting married without using crutches or even a cane. At the hospital the doctors had broken his leg again in order to fix it right and she couldn't imagine the pain of that. But he had practiced and practiced, intent on walking beside her unaided, and she didn't feel that she knew him well enough to assure him, Use the cane, she might have said. Please, Levi, I know your leg bothers you. He was so proud. That was one of his best qualities.

On that very first night in bed with Levi, Rosanna had held still and listened. She had thought he had fallen asleep beside her but how would she know? She tucked the covers around her neck and lay with her arms straight at her sides, watching the shadows play against the edge of the ceiling as sticky liquid ran down the insides of her thighs. The November air outside was cool, very nearly cold, but Levi explained he had to have fresh air in order to sleep, even in winter and it was something she'd have to get used to.

She closed her eyes and tried to sleep but she couldn't stop thinking about her wedding day. My wedding day, she mouthed the words. Her favorite part had been the ceremony itself in the Millers' house next door to her parents' house. She had liked that best mostly because there weren't many people there, just their families and three couples who were their attendants. Levi's father had always been a minister to Rosanna and now he would be her father-in-law, too, just as Levi's grandfather had always been the bishop.

The bishop asked his grandson, Are you confident that this, our sister, is ordained of God to be your wedding wife?

Levi said, Yes.

The bishop turned to her and asked, Are you confident that this, our brother, is ordained of God to be your wedding husband?

Yes, she said shyly.

Then he asked Levi, Do you promise your wedded wife, before the Lord and his church, that you will nevermore depart from her, but will care for her and cherish her, if bodily sickness comes to her, or in any circumstance which a Christian husband is responsible to care for, until the dear God will again separate you from each other?

Yes, Levi agreed.

And yes, she promised to do the same for him.

Rosanna smiled to realize that going over the wedding vows in her mind had made the stinging between her legs begin to fade. She turned on her side and gazed at her husband. Levi was thick and stocky, strong and muscular from a lifetime of hard work. He was the sixth of eight surviving children born to his parents, and the second son. His nearly black thick course hair framed his handsome face. He had sharp blue eyes and, now that he was married, a dense black beard. Those were their ways, the beard was mandatory after marriage and she knew he didn't particularly like it, but, well, she didn't especially like never being able to cut her hair, either, so there!

Now it was her second summer as his wife, her favorite season, summer, with its soft nighttime breezes and the cicadas trilling, bats soaring, hoot owls calling. But summer was nearly over and she still was not pregnant.

Rosanna wanted to be a good Amish wife and mother, to have babies, to take care of the house and garden. She wanted to take care of Levi; or at least she wanted to want to take care of him. Did she love him? She never thought about it. He was the only man who ever courted her and she liked him. She thought he was a good man but lately he had seemed preoccupied, staring out the window at his parents' house, brooding.

Rosanna flipped over in bed onto her stomach. She tucked her hands over her sharp hipbones. A mockingbird was going through his entire repertoire in the oak tree next door. She thought it was her fault. Maybe she was barren. She didn't think she was. She prayed that she was not. But it was hard to be together with Levi when his parents were right over there across the green grass in the house next door. She couldn't help feeling embarrassed about it even though all married couples did it. Wasn't having a child her only reason for being? But the babies didn't come and she couldn't help that.

She knew Levi was unhappy and she couldn't help that, either. Rosanna was afraid that he'd leave her, though they had never spoken of it. Not that he'd divorce her and get another wife. That wasn't done. The Amish didn't do that. But Levi was just so irritable ever since his brother left the farm. He was restless and snappish. And goodness, what was taking him so long at the outhouse?

Rosanna sat up. The dogs were barking out front. Was someone there? And what was that smell? She'd been aware of it for some time but there were always dank musty smells on the farm and she'd learned to block them out. Something was on the floor; she couldn't quite see it in the dark but she knew there was something there. She got the flashlight and switched it on. Blood. There was blood all over the place. She screamed and tears spurted from her eyes. Immediately she snatched her clothes off the peg and climbed onto the bed to dress. The blood frightened her, just the sight of it. Rosanna stepped hesitantly in her bare feet making her way very carefully over and around the blood drops to the top of the stairs.

Blood covered the stairs. She stood at the top with the flashlight out before her like a dagger or a club and Rosanna took a deep breath. She could be fierce. She had untangled her dog from a fight with a raccoon when she was just twelve. She could be strong. That same year she had held her mother's face above water the time the buggy went off the bridge into the river. She knew her mother couldn't swim and so Rosanna had strapped her arm across her mother's chest as she swam to shore to save both their lives.

Rosanna clamped her lips together tight and made her way down the stairs into the kitchen. Blood was everywhere, all the way down the stairs, across the dining room, the kitchen floor, out the door over the stoop onto the gravel drive, trickling over the blue rocks to the center where it ended in pool. The dogs jumped in circles around it barking, hardly pausing to acknowledge her. In fact the sight of her with the flashlight only caused the dogs to increase their racket. Rosanna shone the flashlight on the blood pool for the longest moment. She cast light behind and around it, all the way to the other side of the drive. There was no more blood. It stopped there in a pool. She ran to the outhouse looking for Levi, calling his name. She pushed open the door. It was empty. Rosanna screamed again and swung around, running as fast as she could to his parents' house. She knocked on the window and then she ran inside and pounded on their bedroom door.

The door flew open and Levi's father Joe stood there with an angry face that switched to astonishment when he saw her there. "Rosanna, what is it?"

"Levi's gone. There's blood everywhere."

"What?" Joe nearly bellowed. Levi's mother Katie peered from behind her husband, her mouth in an anguished Oh! There was a lot of scrambling as Levi's sisters and brother ran downstairs and stopped at the bottom in a bunch. Suddenly everyone was following Levi's father through the house to the drive out front, to the puddle of blood, still being circled by the barking dogs. Joe ordered the dogs away with a gruff, "Out!" Then he shined his flashlight along the bloody trail to the kitchen door. It was a horrible scene. Rosanna felt sick to her stomach but she was oddly relieved to have Joe there taking over. She watched her father-in-law follow the lit blood trail into the house, she heard him tromp across the wooden floor, and upstairs to their bedroom. He was back out in seconds.

"Katie," he told his wife. "I'm going to the neighbors' to call the police." He ran. He didn't take the time to get his horse and buggy. He flat-out ran across the drive past the woodshop and the outhouse toward the corn field and disappeared.

Nobody else had moved. Edna, Susie, Sarah, Rebecca and Daniel all clumped in a bunch at the edge of the grass. Their mother, Katie, hovered by the pool of blood, staring at it as if to will it away. Rosanna leaned against the clothesline pole, separate from them, from her husband's family, and she longed for her parents to be there beside her. She was careful not to get too close to the splattered blood as she stood starkly, arms crossed over her chest, small hands balled up into a single wishful fist.

There was commotion all around. The dogs had followed Levi's father but the cows and horses were bellowing and whinnying from the barn. The rooster was crowing even though it was far from dawn. The chickens were squabbling. Cats were all about acting agitated and afraid, jumpy, skittish, sometimes shrieking at one another and spitting, swiping with their claws and dashing away. Levi's siblings were huddled together with their mother, talking and crying when the dogs bounded back and chased each other and the cats.

A car roared up the drive sometime later, a red Jeep. It was quickly surrounded by barking dogs that quieted down instantly when Levi's father got out of the passenger seat. A woman had driven him over. Rosanna thought it might be one of the daughters or daughters-in-law from the farm next door—the woman at the wheel was too young to be Mrs. Handall. She didn't get out of the car and she didn't even wave to Levi's mother. She just backed around and drove out much more slowly.

After a long time there were sirens. The dogs began to howl. "Daniel," his father said. "Put the dogs in the house." Little Daniel collared the two friendly dogs and ran with them over to his parents' house. "Susie," her father said. "You and Rebecca go inside, too." The two youngest girls did what their father said, while Edna, the oldest, stuck by her mother.

Two police cars slid to a halt on the gravel drive. Levi's father met the first car before the men even got out of the cruiser. He leaned in toward the open window and spoke quietly, then moved back while the officers consulted with each other. A long moment later, the first two policemen followed Levi's father along the blood trail up the porch stairs, through the kitchen and upstairs to the bedside of Levi and Rosanna's house, while the other two began stringing plastic crime tape all around the house and drive.

The one policeman who appeared to be in charge went back to his car and got on the radio. Levi's father came up to Rosanna and said, "The police officer wants to talk to you. Let's go into our house. Katie?" he said to his wife. "You and Edna make some coffee. The rest of you try to go back to bed." He gestured to the four youngest who had come back outside and were clustered on the porch. "It's going to be a long night."

Rosanna stood stiffly against the wall and kept swiping the continuous tear that trailed from the outside corner of her right eye; just the right one. Was there some significance to that? That Levi slept on her right? She shook her head to dispel the silly thought. Outside she could hear horses trotting up the drive. The brethren were arriving in masses. The men always came first and she hoped her father was amongst them, even as it was really her mother that she wanted.

The man in charge tried to smile toward her in a kindly way, but his expression remained tense and strained. "I'm Lieutenant Burkhart," he said, motioning for her to sit down at the kitchen table. Rosanna slid onto the bench against the wall. She tugged at the top of her dress in an effort to close it more securely. Her hand flew to her head then. She wore no covering! She glanced sharply at Levi's mother, but the older woman's teary eyes were lowered as she filled cups with coffee.

"Can you explain to me what happened tonight?" he asked.

Rosanna cleared her throat but kept her head lowered. She couldn't look at the man, she wasn't wearing a covering. She crossed her ankles under the table and pulled her skirt down over her legs hoping no one would notice she was barefoot. She stole a glance at Edna and their eyes met. She noticed then that Edna was in her nightgown and her head was bare, too, Edna who was even older than Rosanna. So it was okay then. But it didn't feel okay.

"I woke up with a start. Levi was gone and I smelled something; I sensed there was something on the floor. I got the flashlight and saw that blood was everywhere. Downstairs, too, and all the doors were open." She shook her head nervously and gave an abrupt tight shrug with her shoulders as if to say, that's all I know and it's horrible.

"Did you notice anything missing? Was anything disturbed?"

"I don't think so. Except for the blood."

He looked to Joe and said, "Can we get some more light in here?" Joe motioned to Daniel and Levi's brother lit some more lanterns. The police officer turned back to Rosanna. "And you didn't hear anything?"

"No, no. Not until the dogs started barking."

Outside there were more sirens, distant at first. The dogs' howling was quickly drowned out and the sirens were upon them, unbelievably loud. There were twirling lights, blinking lights, blue, red, and flashing white spot lights. "The fire department has arrived," Joe said from the doorway.

The officer stood up and offered Rosanna his hand. "I want you to come next door with me and walk me through it. You might notice something amiss in the process."

She stared at him wide-eyed as she placed her hand in his, allowed him to help her up, and walked with him to the door, willing herself not to pull her hand away. When Joe said, "Go on, Rosanna," she let her hand fall away and led the policeman across the grass. She was aware of a crowd standing by, brethren, firemen and police, but she kept her eyes forward, numbly making her way past the blood and into her house. That was when she immediately noticed that Levi's glasses were gone from the table. Every single night of their marriage he would take off his glasses and put them on the table before climbing the stairs to bed, and they were gone. But who's to say he didn't put them on when he went to the outhouse—if he had gone to the outhouse. She had a feeling then, perhaps she'd had it from the beginning, a suspicion, an inkling that things weren't what they seemed; her intuition was uncanny and just as she acknowledged that fact, her eyes dried up. The officer told her to go on back to her parents' house and she didn't correct him but hurried across the grass and into Levi's parents' kitchen with Edna. She accepted the cup of coffee and was comforted by the hot mug in her hands though she never took a sip until it was cold.

They were up all night. Rosanna stayed at the table holding the cup of coffee Edna had brought to her. Joe and Katie and the police lieutenant hurried outside. Little Daniel, Levi's brother ran outside, too, even though Edna told him not to. The women waited there, Edna and Rosanna, two sisters-in-law who didn't know what to say to each other.

Daniel came back later and said, excitedly, "Volunteer firemen are walking the Handall's corn field. A local airplane pilot is going to search from the air as soon as it's daylight." His eyes were bugged out with the thrill of it all.

Rosanna could hardly breathe. She couldn't get a breath.

She really broke down when her mother appeared in the doorway and hurried over to her. Tears just poured down her face the way they used to when she was a little girl. Edna got up from the table and Rosanna's mother slid in beside Rosanna and took her hand tightly as she held up a corner of her apron and dabbed at her daughter's red puffy eyes. After awhile the other women prepared a big breakfast, and Edna took Rosanna upstairs to give her a covering for her head while she herself put on clothes. Her sister-in-law nodded to Rosanna as she said, "It'll be all right. I know it will."

By noon the search had been exhausted, the firemen were gone and only a few policemen remained. That was when Rudy, an Amish man about Levi's age, said loudly, "Maybe this is a joke. He could be at Bob's."

"Who's Bob?" the lieutenant asked.

Joe turned his head sharply. "Bob Lowry?"

Rudy nodded.

Joe grimly told the lieutenant, "He's a logger who sells lumber to our sawmills." And then a shadow of recognition crossed over his eyes. "Why would Levi be there?" he asked Rudy.

"Bob took in another fellow who left the Amish, Emmanuel Miller," Rudy replied nervously.

There was a dreadful moment of silence as everyone turned to Joe. "Levi would never leave the Amish!" Joe bellowed.

Rosanna's mother squeezed her hand as Levi's aunt who was standing right in front of them remarked, "I thought if anyone would leave it would be Samuel." Her voice was barely audible.

Rosanna was happy to be hidden in a crowd, especially that day. She looked across the huddle of men to Levi's brother, Samuel. He was talking quietly to Eli Holder, a man about his age. She bit her lips to keep from sobbing out loud.

Three

Sunday morning Levi was awake before dawn as always. He stiffly climbed out the car window, stretched and limped down to the road and stood there. He looked to the left, toward the gas station and home. Boy wouldn't he give just about anything to be sitting down at the breakfast table right about then. He could taste the biscuits and gravy, the Farina. Breakfast, his favorite meal for now and forever, he thought with a rueful shrug. He started walking north, ignoring his hunger. He didn't consider for an instant going back there, though he wished he had thought enough to pack a little food, just in case.

    Before he got to Dale Rammel's place he would have to decide what he was going to do. The Rammels knew him; they were Amish. He walked purposefully up the side of the road scuffing his boots against loose stones and dirt. He kicked a plastic Pepsi bottle into the brush. Down in the gully he saw an entire six-pack of empty Rolling Rock beer bottles and a balled-up bag from McDonald's.

    Around the bend Dale's silo peeked up above the treetops. It looked to be another half mile or so. He stopped in the road, stroked his beard, and then stuck his hands in his pants pockets. The English pants were meant for this. The pockets were deep and angled and the fabric was loose and soft. He felt the folded bills, the quarters, nickels, dimes and pennies he had carefully secreted away, and he smiled sadly. It was so foreign! He couldn't believe that he actually missed the tiny pocket for his watch and the long narrow pockets for pliers. His Amish pants were purposeful. The English pants had just three pockets, one wide deep pocket on each leg for jamming your hands in and for keeping your money, and a small square pocket at the back with a button. What in the world was the button for?

Levi chewed his bottom lip and considered his options: go home or make a bold move. There was no way he was going home. He couldn't wait to shave the beard, to cut his hair. He suddenly remembered another Amish man, Emmanuel, who had left recently, who was living with Bob Lowry, a logger who sold logs to the Amish who have sawmills. Levi decided he'd call Emmanuel. He knew Bob's phone number. He'd stop at the next English house he came to and ask to use the phone. He hoped they wouldn't know he was Amish because an Amish man would only use the phone on Sunday morning if it were an emergency.

He started walking again, a little faster, his spirits lifting with his new plan. There was a white picket fence a short distance away that surrounded a little red-painted cottage, probably one of those vacation kit houses he'd heard about (laughed about really—they were so poorly made). The mailbox was painted red like the house, with big white numbers along the side. A little sign poked out of a patch of red and white petunias at the base of the mailbox: Beware of Dog.

Levi took a deep breath, cautiously opening the gate, and latching it carefully behind him. Then he walked up the brick path to the green door. He hesitated at the sight of a brass knocker in the shape of a dolphin. That took him aback for an instant. He knocked with his hand perhaps a little too softly because nothing happened. Then he lifted the metal dolphin and let it fall back against the door. It made a satisfying clunk. Immediately there was the sound of yapping and toenails scrambling on a hard floor.

"Avery! Avery!" a man's voice commanded. The barking continued, but scrambling noises ceased. The door opened. The man who answered the door seemed pleasant enough. He didn't exactly smile when he saw Levi standing there but he didn't slam the door, either.

He was about fifty with a receding hairline. He had bushy brown hair, and he was a little thick in the middle. He wore a white undershirt and a pair of brown cloth pants. His feet were bare and the toenail on his left-side big toe was black and getting ready to peel off. The shaggy little dog he clutched tightly under one arm squirmed and growled and snapped his little trap jaws at Levi.

Levi had to raise his voice to be heard. "Could I use your telephone?"

"Sure, but if you know the Brewers' score don't tell me. I taped the game." The man waved him in and didn't seem to care one way or another who he was or what he looked like. "Phone's over there." He nodded toward the kitchen wall as he lost his hold on the wiggling dog that was still making a mighty racket. The dog shot to the floor and tore around Levi's boots nipping and snarling. The man snatched the dog up and went down a little hall. The barking stopped.

Levi called Bob's. A woman answered and he asked to speak to Emmanuel. "Here's the deal," he said when Emmanuel came to the phone. "This is Levi. I ran away. Can you come pick me up out in front of Dale Rammel's?" Dale Rammel lived about nine or ten miles from Bob, and Levi was just down the road from Dale's.

Emmanuel said he had to talk to Bob and he put the phone down. Levi shifted from foot to foot and began to feel worried. A TV was on in the room down the hall. "Sign up now and pay only twelve ninety-five. Call the number on your television screen." Then a man half-sang, half-yelled about the Gospel of Matthew, organ music swelled up, and a lot of people began to sing, "A mighty fortress is our Lord." Levi began to chip away at some hardened dirt on his shirt sleeve. A church service on television, that was unbelievable.

Finally Emmanuel was back. "Bob and I will be there in about half an hour," he said.

Levi thanked him, hung up and mopped his forehead with the cuff of his shirt. It had been a long night, even though it was officially morning. He called a thank you to the man down the hallway, and left the red cottage, closing the door to the sound of barking and four doggie feet running and slipping and sliding down the hall after him. Just as he pulled the door tight against the jamb, he heard the dog throw himself at it with a thud and a flurry of snarls. Levi quickened his step, letting himself out of the gate, latching it securely once again behind him, and walked at a fast clip down the road toward Dale's front drive. He tried to correct his uneven gait but his leg ached intensely and it was impossible not to limp.

He sat down out of sight about twenty feet from the entrance to Dale's front drive, huddled in the shrubs in a copse of scraggly trees. He waited for what seemed like a very long time. He began to worry that they weren't coming. What was he going to do now? Not a single car went by. He tried to guess the time from the position of the sun in the sky, seven or eight? It was going to be a hot one. The back of his shirt was already sticking to him, the bugs starting to stir in the brush. His stomach hurt. His leg was stiff and torn through with cramps. And then there it was, the sound of a rumbling truck coming over the rise on the other side of Dale's.

Levi pushed himself up from the ground, brushed off the seat of his pants, rubbed his sore leg, and straightened his slacks, pulling the cuffs down over the tops of his boots. He stepped out of the tree line just as a big white pick-up truck pulled over in front of Dale's. A loud black dog was loose in the truck bed, barking his head off as Levi approached. There were two men in the truck, but where was Emmanuel? Levi hesitated just as the passenger door opened and a guy hopped down, waving broadly. Levi barely recognized him. Emmanuel wasn't wearing a hat and his blond hair was cut so short he looked practically bald. He wore blue jeans from the store and a T-shirt that said University of Wisconsin. Levi was so surprised to see Emmanuel in English clothes he walked right up to the truck and nearly got his hand bit off by the big black dog that lunged at him with an open mouth full of sharp white teeth.

"This is Bob's dog, Lucky," Emmanuel said. "Hold your hand out palm down, let him smell you, and you should be okay." Levi did as he was told, noting that Bob had a hold on the dog's collar through the back window of the cab.

When he got in beside Emmanuel, he thanked Bob immediately and pulled the heavy door shut. Bob let go of the dog, started up the truck, and did a U-turn. Then they just roared up the road. With the windows open they wouldn't have been able to hear one another even if Levi could think of something to say. He put his elbow out the window the way he saw Bob doing. Bob's gold wedding band sparkled and flashed on his large hand. The ring looked out of place on him. Levi had known Bob Lowry was a big man but up close like that it was hard not to stare. His head came right up against the roof of the truck cab, flattening the top of his baseball hat, and his knees pressed up against the gear shifts. His right hand on the steering wheel was gigantic, covered in nicks and cuts, but strangely there was no dirt under his fingernails. They were blunt-cut with white curved tips. Levi had never seen such clean fingernails on a man before.

It didn't seem to take any time at all before Bob swung the truck into a wide gravel drive. A huge logging truck and two regular pick-ups, both white just like the one they were in, filled up a pull-off to the left, and Bob kept going up a sharp incline toward a two-story house. They pulled to a stop behind a pale blue mini-van. Bob's house was painted white with dark blue shutters. There was a large picture window looking out over the road, and a low stone wall, about knee-high, that ran all along the front on either side of a stone walkway.

Bob led the way. Levi was behind Emmanuel, who wasn't exactly short, probably about five-eleven. He figured Bob must be about six-foot-six. The door was opened by an attractive woman wearing a very thin silky pale blue blouse—he could clearly see her bra straps—and a short blue and gray checkered skirt, with white sandals on her bare feet. "Laura," Bob said. "This is Levi." Levi smiled nervously as she said hello and asked them in. She was average height, with blond hair pulled back in a knot behind her head and the oddest thing was that she wore pink-tinted eyeglasses.

"Just in time for breakfast," she chirped. "Bob, would you get the boys. Tell them we have to leave in fifteen minutes or we'll be late for church. Emmanuel, would you show Levi where the bathroom is, and also the bedroom. But come right back," she called after them. "I've already pulled the casserole out of the oven. Breakfast is ready. Boys--," she said in a much louder voice. "Breakfast."

Levi followed Emmanuel past a large room with two small sofas (he couldn't imagine Bob sitting on one of those!) facing two matching chairs. Everything was blue. "We're in here," Emmanuel pointed to a room on their left. Levi paused in the open doorway of a small bedroom with twin beds and thick blue carpeting. The blue-checked bedspreads matched the curtains. "The bathroom's here," Emmanuel said over his shoulder as he went a few steps further down the hall and pointed to a closed door. "Peter or John must be in there. They're Bob's boys." He gave Levi a wry grin. "They're hardly boys. They're nearly as tall as Bob and they go logging with him. So do I, and you can, too, if you want, in exchange for room and board."

It was a lot to take in, the carpeting, the painted walls, the basket of red, blue, orange and yellow dried flowers on the shiny table, and a bathroom, inside the house. The hallway walls were lined with large framed photographs of Peter and John throughout the years, starting from when they were little boys up until, he guessed, high school-age. Each photo had the same dusky blue background. He could hardly get his mind off breakfast, though. His stomach was growling, and his mouth was practically watering at the thought of even something as simple as a slice of bread.

They gathered in a white dining room. The table was polished cherry wood and set with dark blue placemats and white plates with little painted blueberries around the rims. John and Peter wore friendly expressions when they were introduced but neither one said a word at breakfast. Levi did what everyone else did. He passed his empty plate to Laura and she spooned out a steaming concoction of eggs and cheese with bits of bacon covering the top. There was a pitcher of orange juice, another pitcher of ice water, and a thermos of coffee.

When Laura served Bob's plate she absolutely heaped on the casserole before handing it to him. He plucked a stack of four pastries off another plate and set them on top of the egg mixture. Laura poured him a full glass of orange juice, which he took, as he passed his mug over to her. She filled it with hot coffee and added two spoonfuls of sugar plus a hefty pour from the cream pitcher. When she handed it back, he stirred it with a spoon and took several long sips, as he sighed loudly, showing his pleasure, which made Laura smile. She served herself a modest amount of eggs and did not take any pastries.

Levi watched and wondered. He was curious to see Laura waiting on Bob just as Rosanna waited on him. Laura had to remind Peter to pass the pastries and Levi took two sugary squares topped with jam. He felt so strange sitting at the table with these new people. The food was so tiny and pretty like a picture and he felt a bit clumsy as he took tiny bites when he really wanted to wolf it down. It all tasted good but he would've eaten just about anything, accustomed as he was to having a big breakfast.

Bob did most of the talking while they ate. It had been a hot summer. They hadn't had much rain. Good for logging, though. Laura and the boys were going to be heading off for church. "We go to the 2X2 ministry, have you heard of it? It's also called The Friends. You're welcome to come next Sunday if you're still here."

"Levi might be interested in attending the convention, Bob," Laura suggested. "Emmanuel, too." She smiled and nodded to each of them in turn. Levi felt a half-smile curl up on his face as he nodded back in kind, even as he wondered what a convention was. He felt like he was being bombarded with new things, but of course that's exactly what was happening.

"Sure!" Bob agreed heartily. "When is that, Laura, the end of September?" He didn't wait for an answer but picked up a pastry, popped it in his mouth, and turned back to Levi, talking with his mouth full. "But if you like, Levi, today Emmanuel and I can show you the ATV trails Peter and John made. We have a couple of 4-wheelers. It's a great day for kicking up some dirt. I suspect you've never driven an ATV."

"No, I haven't, and yes I would like that." Levi didn't exactly know what he was agreeing to but he nodded his head enthusiastically, causing his long hair to bob up and down.

After Laura and the two boys left for church—and Levi didn't envy them that in the least, Bob and Emmanuel led the way out through the kitchen where there was a large deck overlooking a stand of trees. There was a table with a bright blue umbrella, and behind that, a hammock that Levi eyed as they passed it by, it looked very comfortable. Sleeping in the back seat of the junk car had left him with a stiff back. As they approached the wooden stairs that led down off the deck, Levi saw that the deck railing was really a wrap-around bench which he thought was very clever.

Two mud-splattered black 4-wheeled motorbikes sat at odd angles to each other next to a wide dirt trail that disappeared into the thick woods. Levi had seen ones like them on the road, usually in the backs of pick-up trucks or on trailers being pulled by trucks or cars. Men didn't drive them around the way they did cars and trucks but they did take them to town from time to time, and he'd always thought they looked a little silly, a great big person straddling what appeared to be a supersized toy bike.

Bob put his fingers to his mouth and let out a loud shrill whistle and soon the black dog came bounding from around the other side of the house and sat down in front of him. He reached down, picked up a chain that was attached to a big metal ring stuck deep in the ground. As he hooked up the dog, he patted him on the head and said, "It's for your own good, buddy."

Then he went on down to the closest bike and climbed on. "These are automatics," he said to Levi. "Most of the controls are on the handlebars, though this Honda has a brake pedal." He put his right foot on a pedal and clamped his hands onto grips decorated with silver levers and loops of wire. "So, here's the throttle, here's the brake, this key here turns it on but you have to have it in neutral or park." When he touched the key Lucky the dog began a tirade of barking and strained against the chain to break loose.

"Quiet!" Bob bellowed and the dog stopped short. "It's got six gears but go easy on it or it will shoot right out from under you or flip over backwards and roll right over you." He grinned as if he didn't really mean it but Levi took heed of the warning.

Bob got off and motioned for Levi to climb on. He repeated the instructions, going over the controls a second time and then patted Levi on the back. "You're on your own. Emmanuel, lead the way but just take the big loop, don't go off on any of the side trails, and don't let Levi out of your sight for an instant."

Emmanuel straddled the other bike, switched it on and rolled rather slowly onto the dirt trail, idling there until Levi's was in motion. Levi glanced back and saw the dog barking but it was barely audible over the sound of the two motors. He tried as hard as he could to make it run smooth but he lurched and bucked and the machine made alarming grinding noises and finally he made it to Emmanuel stopping with such a jolt he nearly hit his chin on the handlebars.

When Emmanuel revved up and shot forward, Levi followed cautiously going a few times around the loop, and then he was tearing along behind Emmanuel, having the most fun he'd ever had, flying over the dirt trails. Soon he understood how to make the bike speed up and slow down, how to take a turn without sliding or tilting, how not to follow Emmanuel too close, because it hurt when he was pelted with every little thing that was kicked up by Emmanuel's wheels. He tucked in his chin to keep dirt from flying into his eyes but the hardest was keeping his mouth closed, because he couldn't stop laughing and whooping.

He simply marveled at the rumbling power beneath him and the thrill of making it go. Riding a galloping horse was exciting but you bounced around on the saddle and had to keep a grip with your knees and hold tight to the reins and you could never truly trust the animal not to screech to a halt, throw down his head, kick up his rump and launch you headfirst into the hard packed earth. With the bike it was a matter of operating the controls. If he did it right it would work the way he wanted it to. It didn't have its own mind, now did it? Wouldn't his parents just cry to see him right then? There goes Levi off with the devil on a motorbike, he could imagine them saying.

It hardly seemed long at all before Bob came into view with the dog loose by his side. He waved them back and Levi turned around and followed Emmanuel at a respectable distance to park the bike just as he'd found it. He followed Emmanuel into the house to wash up for lunch. The blue mini-van was back out front, and Bob said Laura and the boys were changing out of their church clothes. "Lunch in five," he called.

"That means five minutes," Emmanuel whispered to Levi as he handed him a towel to dry his hands. Bob pulled packages out of the refrigerator and tossed them onto the kitchen table, provolone cheese, honey ham, and something called olive loaf that made Levi wrinkle his nose. Out came jars of mustard, mayonnaise, and two kinds of pickles, all store-bought, plus a loaf of black bread and a bag of white rolls. Peter came in and tore open a large bag of potato chips, put that in the center of the table, and grabbed a handful of knives from the drawer. "Help yourselves," Bob told Emmanuel and Levi.

Then he left the kitchen calling, "Laura? What do you think about hitting the lake this afternoon?"

Levi watched Emmanuel put together a couple of sandwiches and he did the same. He sure would be glad when he wouldn't have to copy every move Emmanuel made but it seemed like a good idea for the time being. He had two ham and cheese sandwiches and a bottle of something green called Gatorade. It was a little too sweet for his taste but John said he lived on it in the summer. "It gets its name from the Gators, the University of Florida football team. It was developed for the team to keep them from getting dehydrated," John explained as he leaned back in his chair, opened the refrigerator and grabbed another bottle of Gatorade from the door inside the refrigerator.

Levi wasn't sure what that word meant—dehydrated. Did it keep the team from shrinking maybe?

Bob and Laura came into the kitchen then and Laura asked John not to drink all the Gatorade in one day and Bob told him not to lean back in his chair. "Four on the floor," he called out. John raised one eyebrow at Levi and Emmanuel and said, "He thinks that's so witty. It means all four chair legs on the floor. Ha ha, Dad. That's what my third grade teacher used to say."

"Where do you think I learned it from?" Bob laughed in return.

Levi finished his sandwiches and pushed his chair back. He watched Laura take out two white buns, pull them apart to open them up, spread mustard and mayonnaise on both sides, then stack up several slices of ham, cheese and olive loaf—whatever that was and it didn't sound tasty to Levi at all. She rolled the thick stack up tight, made three more just like it, and put two fat rolls of sandwich filling on each bun, closed them up, mashed them with her hand, and put them on a plate for Bob. "Ah, it's great to be alive!" Bob said as he bit into the first one.

Levi didn't see Laura eat anything. She pulled a can of something called Slim Fast out of the refrigerator, opened it with a bottle opener, and sipped it. They were just finishing their sandwiches when a lot of ferocious-sounding barking kicked up out front. Peter jumped up and went to the window. "Dad, there's a cop out there and Lucky's trying to kill him."

Levi sat up straight, his eyes opened wide; he swallowed the lump in his throat and licked his lips. A rush of cold air seemed to be rising inside him and he held himself perfectly stiff.

"Dad, hurry," Peter cried. "He's going for his Mace."

Bob jumped up so fast his chair tipped over backwards and he charged outside shouting, "Lucky, come!" The boys and Laura ran after him and stopped right behind him. Levi got up so he could see, but his thigh cramped up something terrible and he bit his lips to keep from crying out. He limped over to the front hall and hovered there trying to rub the pain out of his leg as he warily eyed the scene out front. He saw the dog lunge one final time, before running up to sit in front of Bob. Bob said, "Put away the Mace, officer. It's not going to be pretty if you don't."

Levi relaxed a bit then. The way Bob talked to the cop made him feel safe.

The officer dropped his hand to his side. "Is there a guy named Levi Hochstetler here?" he asked.

Levi stiffened up at the sound of his name. He was shielded from view by Peter and John who were nearly as big as their father. He thought at any second he might just take off through the kitchen door and get lost in the woods but he didn't move. He kept his stance there at the edge of the doorway. His hands were locked together behind his back as if to hold himself in place. Emmanuel had backed away further toward the bedroom as if he were afraid of being caught as well. Laura was behind Levi. She put her hand on his shoulder.

Bob called out, "Yeah, he's here." He ducked his head back in the door, peered past his sons to Levi and said, "Go on out and talk to him. It'll be okay."

Levi was in his socks. Bob had asked them to leave their dirty boots outside when they came in from riding the trails. He looked down at the mud splatters on his English pants and the threadbare toes of his socks. Then he went out there, having to step around the dog that growled every time the cop moved a muscle.

He stopped about three feet away. He didn't know what Mace was but he didn't want to find out, either. "I'm Levi Hochstetler," he said.

The cop's uniform was rumpled as if he'd been up all night. He looked up at the dog, who growled in turn, then put the little bottle he was holding in a slot on his wide leather belt. "You decided to leave the Amish?"

Levi said, "Yeah."

The cop looked him up and down. He was middle-aged, a little soft in the face, with pudgy hands. His expression was more curious than suspicious. "What was the blood you used?"

"Cow blood." Levi folded his arms across his chest. He did not shift his eyes one bit, wanting to appear steady and truthful. But he couldn't stop his eyebrows from bunching up worriedly, and his head began to hurt from the tension.

"Why did you make it look like a crime scene?" the cop asked. He had his hands in his pockets and he was jingling change or keys or something. Bob's dog was barely whining from the front porch as if to ask Bob, let me get him, please-please?

"I wanted them to think I was dead," Levi answered. "That I no longer exist so they don't come looking for me and bring me back." Levi rubbed the back of his neck and pulled the collar away. He had never worn a shirt with a collar before. He didn't much like the tight scratchy feel of it.

The cop looked up at Bob, and Levi did, too, as if Bob would be the judge. He was so huge you would guess he could lift one of those 4-wheelers up with his bare hands and toss it into the back of the pick-up for the ride up to the lumber site. He completely filled up the doorway.

The dog beside him was strangely quiet at last, but his ruff was up and his shoulders quivered.

The cop got into his cruiser, shut the door and put his elbow out the window as he turned back to Levi and said, "If you had hurt someone I would have to take you in." He picked up a little black boxy object on a cord and said, "I found him." Then he started the motor and pulled away, leaving a dust cloud in his wake.

Levi watched the police car until it was out of sight before turning back to the house. Only the dog was there, stretched out on the top step, head on his paws, eyes closed. Everyone had gone inside and Levi was glad of that. He still felt shaky from answering the cop's questions and he didn't think he could stand facing the others just yet. He decided to go around to the back of the house to the deck where his boots were. He had felt so foolish in his socks out there talking to the cop.

He skirted by the front steps keeping an eye on the sleeping dog. He definitely wasn't in the mood to fend off that dog, either, even if he had appreciated the way Lucky took on the cop. If Bob hadn't called him off Levi didn't know what would have happened. The cop might have shot the dog with the mace, whatever that was, or worse. He could have shot the dog with his gun.

Four

Levi walked through a small swath of dried-up lawn to the narrow dirt path that led around back. It was covered in paw prints with tiny piles of shriveled up worms here and there. The land was parched. At home he and his father would be talking about watering the corn before it was too late. They had a tank that held twenty buckets of water that sat on a wagon pulled by a team of draft horses. Walking along the rows while the water dribbled out could take all day. That was another thing he wouldn't miss.

There were two fair-sized windows on that side of Bob's house, with a small window in between. The little one was probably the bathroom window, which meant the others were John's and Peter's bedroom windows. John and Peter had Biblical names and the family went to church, but so far that was the only thing they had in common with Levi. The way they kidded around with their father made him feel a little sad. When was the last time he had laughed with his dad? He couldn't recall.

All the curtains were closed and he could hear loud music drifting down. He walked by quietly, not wanting to call any more attention to himself, glad that they had left him alone but he was also concerned that they'd heard what he told the cop. What would they think of a man who would go to such lengths to get away from his family? Levi really did feel ashamed about the blood trail, especially now that the cop would go back and tell his parents and Rosanna he'd done it on purpose so they would think he was dead. He also felt sad knowing how badly they'd all feel. But he wasn't sorry he'd left, he was sad but not sorry, and there was a big difference between the two in his mind.

He wondered if Bob and his family had expected him to get into the backseat of the cruiser obediently, to disappear from their lives never to be heard from again. He hoped that wasn't what they wished he'd done. They seemed to like him, and if they hadn't wanted him there, Bob wouldn't have come to pick him up in front of Rudy's, they wouldn't have fed him so well, and certainly they wouldn't have allowed him to ride that ATV. That's what Emmanuel said it was called, an ATV. Levi mouthed the letters, a TV, and wondered why it was called that. It was nothing like a television.

Levi stood there undecided about what to do. Maybe he should have gone home with the cop. But if it was bad before it would be so much worse now. He could picture poor Rosanna waking up and seeing the blood everywhere, the shock of it. She would have had to go get his parents, and that would have been nearly unbearable for her, to wake them up and tell them that he was gone and there was blood everywhere. His parents would be mortified at having to go to the English for help. Their farm would be overrun with cops. The brethren would arrive in droves.

And now the cop would go back there and say Levi had left on purpose and he wanted his family to think he was dead. No, there was no going back after that.

Up on the deck Levi picked up his boots, noticing that Emmanuel's were gone. He sat down on the top step, took off his socks and shook them out, picked off bits of leaves and dust and dirt that were stuck in the knit. He held his boots out over a little flowerbed and banged the soles together, careful not to let the dirt fall on the pink flowers down below.

"Levi, are you all right?"

Suddenly Laura was right behind him. He stood up abruptly, as if he'd been caught red-handed, and dropped his boots right onto the flowers he'd been trying to avoid. He hurried down the stairs, snatched up the boots and tried to resurrect the bent flower, but when he did, the whole thing came right out of the dirt. He poked it back in the hole and pressed hard shelves of dirt around it, looking up at her worriedly. She had changed into a loose dress covered in sunflowers and the neckline was so low he could see the top of her breasts. He felt his face flush with heat.

Laura laughed and shook her head. "I just can't keep those things watered. Don't worry about it. Did I startle you?" When she leaned over to flick a mosquito off her ankle he could clearly see down the loose neckline to her pink lace bra barely capturing her two pale breasts.

Levi looked away instantly but the image stung his mind with what only could be described as desire and this horrified him. He felt his mouth hanging open and slammed it shut.

"You must be upset being questioned by the police like that, but around here they know all about the Amish. The officer was respectful, wasn't he?"

Levi nodded politely. He supposed the cop was respectful. At least he hadn't been handcuffed and thrown into the backseat of the cruiser. What in the world would his father say if he had to drive the buggy into town and bail his son out of jail? But could you be put in jail for running away? You could be forced to pay for the trouble you caused. He'd heard of that. One of the Yutzy boys had gotten drunk back in the spring and run his buggy into a farm stand. He had to rebuild the stand and pay for the ruined vegetables. And that was just his punishment with the English. Levi could only imagine what the Amish had done to him for drinking alcohol in the first place. Laura was watching him. "I'm sorry about the police coming here to look for me," he offered.

"Oh, Levi, don't worry about that. Bob wouldn't have reached out to you if he was at all concerned about the police."

"Can I ask you something?"

"Of course."

"What exactly is mace?"

"Oh, that's something that burns your eyes like crazy. Police use it to subdue criminals. Which you certainly are not! I think the officer was afraid of Lucky, with good reason." She held out a brown bag. "Now, I went into the attic and gathered up some of John's and Peter's things I think might fit you. We can go shopping tomorrow if you like, but I think there's probably something here you can wear in the meantime. We thought we'd go to the state park. There's a wonderful lake there and a great barbecue place on the way back where we could pick up supper. It's called the Three Little Pigs and it's run by members of our church." She handed him the bag and then went back in the house.

Levi walked up to the kitchen door, stepped out of his untied boots, left them on the deck, and went inside carrying the brown bag. The kitchen was empty. He passed through the living room and saw Bob and Laura and the boys gathered around the mini-van out front. The boys were both shirtless and barefoot and they were wearing bright-colored shorts that came all the way down to their knees. Maybe those were swimsuits. Bob wore a tee shirt and a pair of long dark blue shorts, with white socks and big white clunky sports shoes. Laura was in the sunflower dress but she had a big straw hat on that hung down to her shoulders.

Emmanuel came out of the bathroom wearing the same style of long shorts, only his were brown with yellow stripes and he wore the same University of Wisconsin t-shirt he'd had on before even though it was soaked with sweat and dirty. "Hey," he laughed when he saw Levi looking at his get-up. "Laura has a saying, when in Rome do as the Romans do. These are Peter's swim trunks from when he was in high school. I see she found you some stuff, too."

They went into the bedroom and Levi emptied the bag of clothes on the bed. There were swim shorts like everyone else's, only they were black with a silver stripe down each side. He held them up and saw that they would probably fit, that is assuming he had the nerve to

58

put them on and go outside in front of everyone. He took a deep breath.

Emmanuel took the swim shorts from Levi and opened them up to show Levi the inside. "This is called a built-in jock strap," he said. "Bob told me all about it. It's like underwear only tighter so your stuff doesn't dangle." He handed them back to Levi, and they both laughed a little to cover their embarrassment. Emmanuel went back to sorting through the clothes. He stacked up a pair of Lee blue jeans with two identical University of Wisconsin t-shirts and three pairs of rolled-up white socks.

"Laura says they buy these tee shirts and socks in bulk at the Big Flea. That's an open air market where the English sell everything under the sun."

He put some large rubber sandals that said Nike down on the floor in front of Levi's feet. Then he reached under the other bed and pulled out a similar pair. He dropped them on the floor and slid his bare feet in. "Just like Jesus," he quipped.

Levi had to smile. "Have you been to the lake with them before?"

"Last week. You'll like it. Once you get over the shock of being surrounded by the English."

"What do you do there?"

"Swim and play volleyball."

Levi's spirits practically soared. He'd never had so much fun in one day before. First the four-wheelers, and now swimming and volleyball—in their community they weren't permitted to play volleyball except when they were at home with just the family. He held up the swim shorts. "I guess I should put these on, huh?" He didn't want to put them on. When they swam in the pasture creek they didn't wear anything. But it was just boys, he and his buddies. A wave of regret hit him then. He had broken so many rules just since the night before—it was hard not to think about the consequences; whatever they may be.

Emmanuel stopped in the doorway. "When everything is different all of a sudden it takes some getting used to it. As Bob says, you've just got to wrap your head around it. They understand. I'm not the first Amish they've helped and you won't be the last."

"I saw her." Levi raised his eyebrows guiltily and looked toward the front of the house. He felt the heat spread up through his face all over again.

Emmanuel grinned. "The English are not shy. Laura is genuinely nice and easy to talk to. She's really friendly to everyone. It's okay. I'll go on out and tell them you're changing. And don't worry," he said over his shoulder. "You won't have to confess any of this to anyone."

Thank goodness for that, Levi thought, for surely he'd forged a clear path to hell just in the past half hour. He shook his head in disbelief at the way Laura had leaned over him, touched his arm, spoken softly right into his ear as if she were his wife. He didn't know if he could ever get used to the forwardness of English women.

Levi put on the swim shorts and felt so peculiar. He pulled on one of the T-shirts, and then slipped his bare feet into the rubber sandals. They were surprisingly comfortable. He left his getaway clothes in a wad on the floor. What he'd like to do is to just throw them away. He wondered what Laura would think about that.

In the bathroom Levi caught sight of himself in the mirror over the sink and he burst out laughing. He laughed so hard tears came into his eyes. His hair stood out like a rag doll's and his face was filthy. He used the soap that was in a seashell dish even though it was shaped like a lemon and washed his face clean. Then he wet his hair and tried to flatten it down as best he could. He used the toilet, flushed it, washed his hands again, and before he left he pulled the plastic curtain away from the bathtub and peered up at the big overhead faucet with interest.

English took showers. He wondered if he'd be allowed to take a shower. He hoped Emmanuel knew how to operate the thing so he wouldn't have to worry about looking foolish or breaking it. Although it seemed pretty straightforward, there was a knob that said hot and another one that said cold. What more did you need to know?

When he went outside they were already in the van. Levi climbed into the back seat and sat next to Emmanuel and off they went. If Bob looked silly crammed into his big white pick-up truck, it was even funnier to see him behind the wheel of the mini-van. The whole way there, Laura chattered away. Levi wasn't sure who she was talking to, Bob or the boys, because no one answered her. John and Peter sat in the middle seat, each one wearing something called ear buds that played music right into their brains as far as Levi could tell, and he and Emmanuel were on their own in the back. He stared out the window as woods and farmland flashed by and he thought about Laura's breasts, shook his head swiftly to clear it, and thought of her breasts again, and then he smiled to himself. He knew it was wrong for him to have seen her like that, but she was the one showing him her breasts, so how could he not look on with appreciation?

All at once Levi realized he was content, that was the word for it, and he had never before in his entire life felt that way. There he was in the back seat next to his new buddy, Emmanuel, going to a lake to swim, he loved swimming, and playing volleyball with John and Peter and Emmanuel should be a lot more fun than it was with just his sisters and brothers. But the best part was that no one was expecting anything of him. Rosanna wasn't there searching his eyes to see what kind of mood he was in, his father wasn't reminding him of all the chores he had to do, his mother wasn't fussing and worrying or looking sad.

And just like that his heart sank. Thinking of Rosanna and his parents squashed the feeling of contentedness instantly and Levi decided right there and then that if he had any chance of surviving in this new life he was going to have to learn to block all thoughts of his family from entering his mind.

There were a lot of people at the park. They had to stand in line and go through something called a turnstile. Bob paid and then handed out little plastic tags they had to wear on their wrists or around their ankles. Levi followed Emmanuel, Bob and the boys into the Men's Locker Room, another first. There were all kinds of men and boys in there, mostly white, some Mexican types, a few black ones, and a small group of Chinese-looking ones. He pushed away the automatic flood of cautionary feelings. His parents had taught him from a young age not to feel safe around people who were different. He'd have to get over that now that he was on his own.

The room was a little dark and completely tiled. On one side of the room there were toilets with doors, and on the other, there were big white stand-up toilets just out in the open. "Those are called urinals," Emmanuel whispered to him. "I'm never going to use one of those." Levi nodded in agreement. The next room had a wall with shower heads all along it and there was an old guy in there buck naked. The last room was narrow. It had nothing but metal lockers with benches.

Levi followed behind Emmanuel and the others and they emerged out the other side of the building into the sun. He had to squint until his eyes adjusted to the brightness. The lake and beach was down below. They had to go along a walkway and then descend a long cement staircase. The sand was slightly orange and the lake was brown. There were little groups of people all over the place, some with umbrellas and blankets and chairs.

To the left there were picnic tables and behind that, a white sand pit with a huge net. People of all sizes and shapes were hopping about while a single ball was lobbed from one side to the other. Levi watched for a bit and was happy to see that the game appeared to be the same one he knew how to play.

The beach was fairly large and spaced evenly from one side to the other were three big giant ladder chairs. Each chair had a white ring with a red cross on it, hanging from a rope off the back. There were two people on each chair. Some were sitting, and others were standing, waving and shouting or blowing whistles.

"Those are lifeguards," Peter said as they passed one. "If they blow the whistle on you it's because you're doing something you shouldn't be doing." Levi raised his eyebrows to show he understood. He wouldn't do anything wrong he hoped. Out on the lake, there was a line of small colored floating balls like a fence, dividing swimmers from boaters.

"Once when we were here," John said excitedly. "Everyone had to get out of the water and we formed a human chain."

"Yeah, that was cool," Peter said.

"What's a human chain?" Emmanuel asked.

"A kid was missing and we held hands and walked slowly through the water hoping to trip on him and pull him out and keep him from drowning."

"Did you find him?" Levi asked.

"No, he eventually turned up. He'd gone to buy himself a cheeseburger and he was only five years-old." They laughed.

Bob and Laura spread an Army blanket on the sand near the volleyball net and Laura placed a large bright pink towel on top of that. She sat down and dug a bottle of sun lotion out of her bag. Everyone else kicked off their sandals and pulled off their shirts. Bob's boys ran to the shoreline. Levi and Emmanuel asked if it would be all right if they went swimming, too, and naturally Bob laughed and took off running, calling out behind him, "Last one in is a rotten egg." The whole scene reminded Levi a little bit of a frolic in that there were people everywhere and a lot of talking but that was the only similarity, and Emmanuel was right, he did have fun.

He went in the water and swam out to the string of brightly colored balls floating on a rope. He dove down and touched the bottom. It was silty and a little slimy. The swim shorts didn't bother him at all, though the jock strap itched. The water was over his head in one corner and he swam around there for a bit studying the boats on the other side of the rope. Some were row boats, but the other ones were much larger. Two people were side by side staring straight ahead and their knees were going up and down. Peter swam up beside him and said, "Those are pedal boats."

"Really, kind of like a bicycle?"

"Kind of. We're going to get a volleyball game going after the next break, do you want to play?"

"Sure," Levi said. Just then all of the lifeguards stood up and blew their whistles. The people in the water all headed for shore. "What's happening?" he asked Peter.

"This is a break. You have to get out of the water every hour on the hour so they can make sure no one's drowning. Come on, I'll race you!" Peter swam away in a flash, arm over arm, kicking up a lot of water with his feet. Levi dove underwater and came up beside Peter within seconds. He didn't just try to keep up, he tried to win the race. He was pretty fast himself, and they were both walked out of the water together.

It was the same with volleyball. He caught on almost immediately and enjoyed jumping high to hit the ball when it came near him. Peter showed him how to serve. "You have to stand back here, and don't step over this line." He dragged his toe over a white line. "You hold the ball in this hand, raise it up over your head, aim for the opposite corner on the other side, and hit it with your fist." Levi gave it a try and Peter shouted, "Good serve for your first time, Levi." He didn't let on that he'd played volleyball with his sisters and brothers—since that might as well have been a different game. Siblings don't make up the best team since they're all different sizes and there's a lot of teasing going on. Levi, for one, had always tried to hit the ball over his sisters' heads and he usually did. Then they'd complain that he wasn't playing fair and well, this was a lot more fun. Total strangers came over and joined in the game and it got rowdy but in a good way, with lots of cheering and carrying on.

They left just before sunset and stopped at The Three Little Pigs. Everyone piled in and sat in a booth. Giant plastic glasses were filled with sweet tea almost immediately and after awhile a waitress brought Styrofoam containers with lids. When Levi opened his there was an immense hamburger bun filled with barbeque that spilled out the sides when he bit into it. It was extremely spicy and he had to drink a lot of tea to wash away the burn it left in his mouth but he liked it. Mostly he liked being in a restaurant.

That evening Bob and Laura told Levi he could stay as long as he needed and he could go logging with Bob and the boys and Emmanuel in exchange for meals and having a place to stay. Levi readily agreed, and thanked them. "What will I be doing when we go logging?"

"The boys and I go up the trees in cleats, sheer off limbs and branches and drop them down. You and Emmanuel drag them clear and cut them into smaller pieces and throw them into the truck. Then we saw the limbs in big or smaller pieces depending on the wood. Sometimes we'll need your help holding ropes for leverage. I'll show you how to operate the chain saw. It's not hard."

That night before they went to sleep Levi and Emmanuel sat across from each other on the twin beds and talked quietly. "Have you thought about what you want to do?" Emmanuel asked.

"Yes," Levi said. "First thing, I want to know where to get a haircut like yours and second, I have to shave this beard off. Or maybe it's the other way around. Third, I want to get my driver's license."

Emmanuel laughed and fell back on the bed.

"What's so funny?" Levi was smiling. He thought it was funny, too, the way he'd rattled it all off as if he'd made a list.

Emmanuel sat up. "So you agreed to go logging with us?"

"I think so. You work for him and you get to stay here free and they feed you too? Yeah. Yeah. I want that."

"You know what I would do first?" Emmanuel asked.

"What?"

"I'd go out in the hall and see if the bathroom's free."

"I don't have to go to the bathroom," Levi interrupted him.

"And I'd take a shower, a hot shower. You won't believe it."

Levi's eyes lit up. "You mean now? It's not too late? Do we need to ask?"

"No, it's fine, but don't stay in too long or they might get upset. They have a well, but it costs to heat the water up and it can run out, the hot water that is. John gets yelled at sometimes for staying in there too long."

"Yeah, no, I don't want to get yelled at." Levi got up, opened the bedroom door, and peered out. "The bathroom door is open. The bedroom doors are closed," he said over his shoulder.

"That means the boys are done. Go for it. There are towels in a closet in there. Take one and hang it up when you're done. Sometimes after awhile the towels are all washed and put away and you have to get another one."

Levi went down the hall and into the bathroom. He heard Emmanuel behind him and turned around. Emmanuel handed him the brown bag. "You should put on clean clothes afterwards."

"Okay, thanks."

Emmanuel was right. The hot water pounding on his back was amazing, it felt fantastic, and it was nearly impossible to make himself turn the water off and get out of the shower.

Five

On Sunday, after the search for Levi had ended and the crowd started to break up, Rosanna and her mother walked hand-in-hand back to her house. Edna and Daniel had poured buckets of water over the front steps and swept and swept until the blood dispersed. Inside Katie and some other women had used rags and mops do to the same, but there were tell-tale dark spots everywhere.

"Would you like me to stay the night?" Her mother asked and Rosanna declined, knowing that her father would be put out if his wife did not go home with him, fix his dinner, and sleep beside him as she was supposed to. Here there was just the one bed upstairs, hers and Levi's, and her mother would not be comfortable sleeping beside her in Levi's spot.

"I'll be okay," she assured her mother.

They had lunch at Joe and Katie's, and she watched her parents' buggy pull out just before three o'clock. Edna, prompted by her parents Rosanna was certain, offered to sleep over but Rosanna shook her head, "No. But thank you."

She went home then and tiptoed about eyeing the dark spots where the blood had seeped into the wood, even though she knew the women had cleaned thoroughly. She got a rag and a bucket of soapy water just the same and went over the floors and stairs again and again, until she heard the dogs barking and a car pull up outside. Quickly, she dropped the rag in the bucket and ran to the kitchen window just as the policeman got out of his cruiser and walked up to Joe and Katie's house. Joe stepped out onto the porch and they spoke. Rosanna could see Katie's shadow in the doorway. Then the two men walked around the drive and took down the yellow crime tape which they bundled up and heaped in the back of the police car. The officer got in his cruiser and left, followed by the barking dogs.

Joe stood there and watched until the police car was completely out of sight. The dogs scampered back to his side and sat at attention until he patted each one in turn. They ambled off and Joe removed his hat, ran his hand over his head, replaced the hat, adjusted it, glanced back at his house where Katie was no doubt wringing her hands, and then he trudged across the gravel drive to where he knew Rosanna also waited.

Rosanna dreaded his news. When he passed in front of the window she saw the pained look in his eyes. His mouth was set in a resolute frown. She stood perfectly still. There was the customary knock, then the door opened and he walked into the kitchen. Rosanna's heart pounded in her ears. Here came the tears. She wiped her nose on her wrist and dabbed at her eyes with her knuckles. She tried to compose herself but it was impossible.

Joe said, "Levi is at the logger's. He doesn't want to come back right now."

Rosanna sat down and closed her eyes and a slight smile crept onto her face just to know that Levi was alive. Then she realized Levi was alive and he was not coming home, he had left her on purpose. He had created this terrible mess all over their home and run off in the dark. The smile dropped away almost immediately. She would have to leave, too. She couldn't stay here, not without Levi. She would go home. She had already mentally packed her bags. Her mother had said, No, your place is with your husband's family. But what would they do if she showed up, bar the door?

Suddenly she sprang up from the chair and cried, "What am I going to do now?"

Joe looked upon her kindly. "Rosanna, you'll do what you've always done. Keep house here. Help Katie and the girls. Go to church." He started to leave, and then he stopped and turned around. "How would you like to teach school?"

To have somewhere to go each day, yes, she would like that. She nodded.

"I'll arrange it."

She wanted to hug him, but of course she did not.

Rosanna was the youngest in her family and so there were no siblings to look after when she herself was out of school. She became a teacher when she was sixteen and for one brief season she thought she was doing a good job. Even though she was uncomfortable standing up before so many boys and girls, some of whom were bigger than she was, she worked hard to keep their attention, and when they misbehaved she'd talk to them but she never punished them and this made them disrespect her even more. Yet she never reported them, she just tried harder and hoped they'd come around to liking her.

That was such a lonely time. She felt awkward going to the Young Folks gatherings and sitting by herself, but her mother encouraged her to participate in the hymn sings. When a new girl moved into their community, a tall stately girl named Eva, Rosanna befriended her. Eva was older than the others, not in years, but in manner. She was sophisticated and interesting, and Eva didn't have any friends, either. So they took to sitting together at hymn sings and sometimes they would sneak out and walk around talking about falling in love, something neither of them had experienced, but each wanted very much.

It was during one of their walks that Eva confided in Rosanna that her older brother Amos had been practicing sexual relations on her. Instead of saying, Eva, that's not right, Rosanna wanted to know what it was like and Eva told her everything. One December afternoon Eva was waiting when Rosanna left school. She was crying as she pulled Rosanna aside behind a stand of trees and told her she thought she might be pregnant and she was going to have to end it somehow. Rosanna put her arm around her friend and walked her all the way home and up to her front door. The door opened and Eva's mother glared at them. Eva began to cry again as Rosanna sputtered out her friend's confession. "Eva thinks she's pregnant." Eva was pulled into the house and the door was slammed in Rosanna's face. Rosanna stood there dumbfounded as Eva's sobs turned into screams punctuated by slapping sounds.

The next day Rosanna went to school as usual and at lunch time Rebecca Miller, who had taught several years before and had since gotten married and had a baby, came into the classroom and said, "You should clear out your personal things, Rosanna. You've been replaced. I'll take over for the afternoon."

"But why?" Rosanna tried to search Rebecca's eyes but Rebecca wouldn't look at her when she spoke.

"You have been leaving the hymn sings. As a teacher, it is particularly important that you behave properly."

Rosanna felt her face bloom with heat and embarrassment. She didn't know what to say so she packed up the rest of her lunch grabbed her coat and walked home. Her parents were ashamed of her for losing her job but neither one let on that they knew the details and Rosanna never saw Eva again.

This disturbance from her past defined her in the community. She stopped trying to have friends at Young Folks though she feigned a pleasant attitude. People thought she was stand-offish, and she supposed she was. Her father depended on her more to help out around their farm and her mother let her take on more of the household chores. She began to think that she'd never marry and she'd just live out the rest of her days taking care of her parents.

When Levi started courting her she was grateful and when they married she was determined to do anything to please him. When he left, she assumed it was because of her.

She slept alone in their marriage bed for the first time that night and woke up to the sound of Joe's horse and buggy passing by the open window. It was broad daylight and the day loomed before her causing a bubble of fear in her heart that she simply could not tolerate. But it was Monday, Wash Day, and the hours passed dutifully, surrounded as she was by Katie and Edna and the little ones. She ate by herself that night, though she knew she was welcome at their table. She was afraid her voice would shake if she said anything at all, or the tears would burst from her eyes at the sight of Levi's favorite mashed potatoes or biscuits and gravy.

On Tuesday, Rosanna intercepted Edna as she was coming from the henhouse carrying two large baskets of eggs. "I'll do the farm stand today," she offered, not waiting for an answer as she reached for the baskets, clasping each handle tightly, straining just a bit at the weight of the large baskets brimming with brown eggs.

Edna opened her mouth as if to protest, since stocking the farm stand was her job, and she enjoyed being out there conversing with Amish and English alike, and later telling tales of the gossip she overheard or describing the outlandish outfits worn by the English. Rosanna could tell from the look on Edna's face, that she had really wanted to get away from the house for awhile, but she allowed Rosanna to take the eggs, and it dawned on Rosanna that she had just behaved in a new way toward her sister-in-law. She had been forceful, not taking no for an answer, and Edna had been startled into letting her have her way as if she—Rosanna—was unpredictable now, and maybe even fragile. Being the wife whose husband left her did grant Rosanna certain privileges, at least for the time being, and she was going to need to take advantage of her new standing, simply in order to get from one day to the next.

She smiled her thanks and walked up the farm lane to the road. Brushed off the wooden farm table, opened the cash box and organized the bills and coins, straightened the large Eggs for Sale sign propped up against the table leg. Within moments, she saw the red Jeep approach, the same one that had brought Joe back from the neighbor's when he went to call the police on Saturday night, and the driver was the same, as well, the woman who was much too young to be Mrs. Handall, whom Rosanna had met a few times when she came by, once to ask about ordering bookshelves, another time to see if Joe would be able to make new side pieces for her antique bed.

This time the woman in the Jeep parked in the dirt and got out of the car, talking loudly as she approached the farm stand as if she thought Rosanna was hard of hearing. "Hi, I'm Mallory Handall, Jerry's cousin, from next door? I know Edna."

"Yes," Rosanna replied. The English were always so bold. She blinked a few times in case her expression revealed anything like surprise at the lack of clothing the woman wore—a top that was so tight it was obvious she wasn't wearing a bra, and so scant as to perfectly expose her smooth brown stomach with a red gem flashing where her belly button should be. Her short denims were frayed to a fine fringe not too far from her crotch and from there on down it was lots of bare smooth-as-wax leg. Rosanna lowered her eyes not so quickly as to appear subservient, but more to indicate she was tending to her task of quickly filling two egg cartons. She re-stacked the empty cartons but kept her hands on them to steady the shaking.

The other woman picked up a carton of eggs and placed two quarters in the saucer. "I don't know if you read," she stammered.

Rosanna looked at her directly, "Of course I read, I'm a teacher." Well, she had been a teacher, and she was going to be again soon. Not that it was this woman's business.

"No, no," the English woman laughed nervously, shaking her head in embarrassment, and biting her lips, leaving a pink smudge of lipstick on her front tooth. "I meant, I don't know if you read the newspaper, The Milwaukee Journal? But I saw this article and I cut it out, just in case you wanted it."

She let a piece of newspaper drift onto the tabletop and finished in a rush. "Thank you for the eggs. Bye." She hurried back to the Jeep, her long brown legs sparkling in the sun, her yellow flip flops smacking the dirt, causing bits of gravel and dust to fly up behind her. When she turned on the engine loud music blared for an instant. "Sorry about that," she called out and drove off, trailing a dust cloud along the shoulder before jutting up onto the asphalt.

It all happened so fast Rosanna was momentarily astonished, and still bothered by the woman's inappropriate clothing. It was hard to stand before a woman who wore shorts like that out in public. In fact, Rosanna found it hard to trust women who did not wear skirts. She leaned across the table, pinned the newspaper article down with one finger, and read it through quickly without taking a breath.

Milwaukee Journal Sentinel August 27, 1996
Police say Amish man faked abduction

Eau Claire – An Amish man was found safe after faking his own abduction by spreading cow blood around his bedroom in an effort to abandon the Amish community, authorities said Monday.

Apparently the ploy worked, because the man's father told officials he has now been banished from the Amish community. Authorities found Levi Hochstetler, 21, of Augusta, Sunday afternoon in a rural Jackson County home. More than 30 officials and citizens had searched by ground and air since he was reported missing Saturday, said Eau Claire County sheriff's investigator John Vogler.

Vogler said Hochstetler scattered cow blood around his bedroom, dining room and kitchen to make it look as if he was taken against his will.

Hochstetler, who had not had any problems within the Amish community, did not give a reason for wanting to leave the Amish faith, Vogler said.

Hochstetler's father told Vogler that his family and the Amish community would no longer have anything to do with him.

Seeing Levi's name in print like that filled her with a rather frightening combination of fear and pride. Rosanna straightened up and stood back, gazed up and down the road and then checked the lane behind her. No one was about. No one knew she had the article, no one, that is, but the Handall cousin who had given it to her, and based upon that woman's nervous manner, Rosanna doubted she'd tell anyone, least of all anyone in the Amish community. She carefully folded and refolded the newspaper article until it was a small square tab, tucked it into her apron waistband, and then walked straight back to her house, inside, and upstairs to sit on the edge of her bed, contemplating what to do. After awhile, she took the little square of newsprint and placed it under the dusty ball of lavender soap wedged behind the base of the bed. Then Rosanna curled up against her pillow, hands in a prayer position, and fell asleep.

August was endless and then it was September and Rosanna left every morning and walked to the schoolhouse. She supervised eleven students, many bigger than she, like before, but marriage had made her stronger. Her students did what she said without sneering or arguing and she began to feel confident. Her favorite times were morning prayers and hymns, recess, lunch, and reading aloud. She didn't want to get into any trouble with the Amish so she only read aloud from the Book of Proverbs. She wasn't a very good teacher, she knew, as she hadn't been a very good student, but no one misbehaved or complained, and for that she was immensely relieved.

This went on for two months and she no longer cried herself to sleep at night or wondered what she was going to do or whether she'd ever hear from Levi again. She even began to enjoy living by herself. And then, at the end of October, just like that, everything changed.

It was a brilliant sunny Saturday. Rosanna was eating lunch alone at her kitchen table, slices of Velveeta and pieces of apple, when a flash of light from the drive caught her attention. She looked up just as a taxi passed by and stopped in front of Katie and Joe's. No one was there. Katie was at a frolic serving lunch, and Edna and the little ones had gone with her. Joe was in the workshop, she could hear him hammering.

Rosanna jumped up and ran to the doorway to stand watch and wait for Joe to appear. The taxi driver got out and shielded his eyes with his hand as he looked from one house to the other. When the hammering continued, Rosanna went out to see what the man wanted. He called to her as she came down the front steps.

"I have a message for Rosanna Hochstetler."

"I am Rosanna."

He thrust a slip of folded notebook paper at her, got back in the car, and began to back it around. Joe was heading out as the taxi was pulling down the drive.

"What is it, Rosanna?"

She unfolded the note and began to read: Levi wants to talk to you. The phone number next to the short message was long distance. She gave the note to Joe, he read it, looked up, and seared her with his eyes. She saw hope there and she felt it in her heart.

"I'll get the buggy hitched up."

They drove to the Amish-built phone shed outside the taxi driver's house. Joe punched in the numbers and handed the phone to her abruptly. A woman answered with a cheery hello.

"This is Rosanna Hochstetler," she said with a scratchy voice. She cleared her throat. "Levi's wife."

"Oh yes, hold on a minute. He's out on the tractor."

Rosanna looked up at Joe. "Levi is on a tractor!" Joe raised his eyebrows in astonishment. Rosanna pressed the receiver to her ear and waited urgently through the long silence. By the time she heard voices and footsteps on the other end of the receiver, her heart was racing. A chair scraped back, there was a clunk, and then he was there. "This is Levi."

"Hi," was all she could muster. She felt Joe's hand on her arm. The chair scraping back was for her. He motioned for her to sit down and she did, but her back was straight as an arrow.

Levi told her everything in a rush. "I stayed with Bob and his family and a buddy, Emmanuel, and my first day there we rode motor bikes on dirt trails, swam in a public lake and had barbecue at a restaurant! My first Wednesday there, Bob took me to the DMV, I took the driving test and passed, Rosanna. I got a learner's permit just three days after I left the Amish."

"Three days," she whispered, mesmerized by the energy in his voice.

"Emmanuel and I went logging with Bob and his two boys, John and Peter, for two months. I was using a chain saw. It cuts like a miracle!"

"A chain saw?" She didn't know what that was.

"We worked in exchange for room and board, it was a good deal. One day at the end of September we went to a church convention of the 2X2 ministry, it's also called The Friends. There must have been five hundred to a thousand people there. I met a couple named Doug and Ellen Gainsville from Prairie du Sac—that's where I am now. It's about three hours away. They told me they had a job for me, farm work, a thousand dollars a month plus housing. I say, I'm there. I took my belongings and moved to the farm." Finally he paused to catch his breath.

"You are making a thousand dollars a month?"

"Tell him he needs to come home," Joe said.

"Dad's there with you?" Levi's jovial tone had fallen a few notches to worried.

"Ask him to visit," Joe said.

Levi answered, "No, no tell him I can't do that."

Rosanna tucked her chin in and turned slightly away from her father-in-law so that she couldn't see his face. She spoke quietly into the phone. "Why did you want me to call you, Levi?"

His voice got quiet, too, even intimate. "Doug and Ellen were very curious when they found out I was married. They thought it would be nice for me to be in contact with you, Rosanna. It took some convincing but after awhile, I called the local taxi back home, and asked the driver to deliver a message to you."

Joe took the phone away from Rosanna. "Levi, we'd like for you to come and visit."

Levi said something, she didn't hear what it was, but after a bit Joe handed the phone back to Rosanna. "I think he's considering it."

"Levi?" she said into the phone. He wasn't there, but she heard muffled voices. She looked up at Joe fearfully.

Suddenly Levi was back on the line. "Dad," he said.

"This is Rosanna," she told him.

"Oh. Well, Doug and Ellen don't think it's a good idea for me to come there, but they say you are welcome to visit me here."

"Tell that to your father." Rosanna handed the phone back to Joe. Levi repeated the invitation and Joe said that they would hire a taxi and be there on Monday.

No one spoke during the entire three-hour taxi ride to Prairie du Sac. Rosanna sat in the third seat of the minivan with her parents. Joe and Katie had the second seat. Her thoughts were crazy as the car sped along the highway. What would he look like, how would he act, would their parents make him come home. She hoped so. That was what she wanted. Finally they turned off the highway. They were on a small two-lane road and the farm seemed easy to find, the driver turned down the drive as if he'd been there before. He pulled up in front of the farmhouse, everyone got out of the car, and then he drove up to a large oak tree and parked.

They stood in an awkward group, the men in front, the women in back. The red-painted front door opened and Levi came outside. Rosanna gasped at the sight of him. He was dressed in English clothes, store bought blue jeans and a green Tee shirt that said Badgers. His hair was cut so short it looked as if he had shaved it off. He didn't have a beard. Her heart closed up. Levi was married, yet he had shaved off his beard. That could only mean he did not want to be married to her. Married Amish men always wore beards. Rosanna put her hand to her mouth.

Katie started crying right away. "I can't believe I'm seeing you in those clothes," she wailed.

Rosanna's father called out, "You are listening to the devil."

Rosanna was stunned. She had no idea what she expected, but the sight of Levi was utterly frightening. He walked up to her and took her hand. "We need to go inside and talk," he told their parents. "Ellen and Doug have gone to town to give us some privacy. You are invited into the kitchen for cookies and juice. It's through this door and to the right." He pulled Rosanna by the hand into the house. She was blinded by her tears and she didn't notice a single thing. She couldn't have told anyone later what the kitchen looked like or the rooms on either side of the hallway. When they got to a bedroom she thought it might be Levi's, because the windows were open even though it was a cool autumn day. Rosanna looked around in a daze. The walls were painted green like new grass and the bedspread was checkered, green and white. They sat down on the bed. She turned to him and right away she blurted out, "Please come home, Levi, things will be different."

"Rosanna, listen, I've been reading the Psalms, let me show you. Look at this." He reached for a fat red book on the table beside the bed, opened it up, and began flipping through pages.

She saw the cover. It said Holy Bible. "Where did you get that?" It looked nothing like their Bible. The letters on the pages were large and there were colored pictures.

"It's Ellen and Doug's. Here it is, now listen: Blessed are those whose way is blameless who walk in the law of the Lord. Blessed are those who keep His testimonies, who seek Him with their whole heart, who also do no wrong but walk in his ways." He closed the book and turned to her. "You see, Rosanna?"

She shook her head and tears budded in her eyes. "What is it you want me to see, Levi?" She glared at the book as if it were evil. It didn't look like their Bible. It didn't sound like their Bible.

He put his hand on her shoulder and gave it a little squeeze. "I'm not trying to upset you, Rosanna. I'm trying to explain something very important. I want you to realize that you don't have to be Amish to live the right kind of life, to do what's right."

"That doesn't mean anything to me, Levi. All I know is that I want you to come back. Please come back, Levi, things will be different."

He stroked her face, the side of her neck, her arm. "I've missed you a lot. I'm sorry for what I did. I didn't think I had any choice about it."

"There was a story about you in The Milwaukee Journal." She gave him a challenging look and his eyes twinkled a bit. She saw the surprise there and the pride. She edged away from him fighting the push-pull of feelings that overwhelmed her. She was comforted by the closeness of Levi, yet horrified by the strangeness of him. He reached for her and they kissed tentatively, only to separate awkwardly when Joe appeared in the doorway.

Joe said: "If we confess our sins, He is faithful and just and will forgive us our sins and purify us from all unrighteousness."

Rosanna stood up, smoothed down her dress, and left abruptly. Joe stepped aside to let her through the doorway. In the kitchen there was an untouched tray of cookies and juice. No one was there. She hurried out front. Her parents were in the van with Katie.

She was about to join them when Joe appeared behind her. "Go talk to him. I think he's ready."

Rosanna went back into the bedroom. Levi had his chin in his hands. He stood up when he saw her. "Levi?" He gazed at her for a long time, then went to the window and stared out. She walked up behind him. "Levi, what did you and your father decide?"

He spoke without turning around to face her. "I resolved to really honestly try to be a good Amish man. Not just outwardly but inwardly as the preachers would want me to be." He turned around and took her hand. "As soon as my hair grows back I'll go through the process of becoming a church member again." This was the Amish way. His appearance had to change back to Amish before he could ask for forgiveness.

"That could take months for your hair to grow out."

"I know it."

"Your hair is so short, did you cut it yourself?"

He ran a hand over his head. "I went to a barbershop. This is called a buzz cut." He opened his arms to her and she went back to him. "I still want to do what is right in Amish eyes, Rosanna." They kissed and Rosanna felt like she was melting inside. But on the edge of that feeling was the awareness that he wasn't the same and never would be again; and neither would she.

After awhile they walked out together and waited for Ellen and Doug to return. It seemed like a long time but the sun was still high in the sky when a rumbling pick-up truck pulled into the driveway. Rosanna waited nervously beside Levi while they watched the pick-up come to a stop, for his friends to get out with their packages. They were very friendly. Levi introduced Rosanna and she nodded shyly at their greetings. Then he explained that he was grateful for the work but he had to go back to the Amish. "Would you give my things to Bob and Laura next time you see them?" Doug and Ellen agreed that they would and Levi said goodbye.

He and Rosanna held hands as they walked to the taxi, but she climbed into the third seat with her parents and he got in the second seat to sit beside his parents. Again, nobody spoke for the long ride home.

Six
The Early Years 1979-1989

Levi was four years-old the first time he thought, I shouldn't be Amish, why am I Amish? It was also during that time that he came to the realization: I'm on my own.

It was during the bitter move from his Grandpa Levi's farm in Clark, Missouri, to his Grandpa Samuel's farm in Augusta, Wisconsin. His family was going to Wisconsin to help establish a new Amish settlement in Augusta where Grandpa Samuel was a bishop. Levi was too young to understand Amish hierarchies or the logistics of establishing a new settlement, he, of course, would go with his family, wherever his parents told him to go, although he would miss his Grandpa Levi.

It started out as a big adventure. The family had gathered out front right after breakfast. Levi's eyes opened wide at the sight of the huge semi-tractor-trailer. It nearly filled up the entire driveway and completely dwarfed the smaller truck that had U-Haul plastered all over the side. There were two men there, drivers, and they were looking at a map together. Levi wanted to see the map, too, and he walked on over to them and stood by, but they paid him no mind. Then the men parted ways, the bigger one climbed into the small U-haul, and the shorter one stepped up into the semi. Engines rumbled and the earth seemed to shake. His mother said goodbye to Grandpa Levi and Grandma Anna and she shepherded Levi's little sisters into the U-Haul. Then his father said goodbye to his parents and walked over to the semi. He opened the door and motioned for Samuel, Anna, Edna, Uncle Enos and Levi to get in. Levi ran after his mother. "I want to ride with you, too," he called out.

His mother said over her shoulder, "Levi there isn't room in here for you. Ride with Samuel and the others."

Levi started to get worked up. "I want to come with you." He felt his grandpa's hand on his shoulder. He shrugged out of his grandpa's grip and rushed at the U-Haul yelling. "I want to come with you."

His mother flew at him with her hand out to give him a swat just as his father snatched him up and carried him to the semi. The door behind the driver's seat hung open and Levi was set down firmly next to his brother Samuel. The door thudded shut. Soon the semi rumbled and roared and trundled out the dirt drive behind the U-Haul that carried his parents.

It was a nine-hour drive to Wisconsin, and Levi sulked and glowered no matter what anybody said to him. Uncle Enos dozed a great deal and would sometimes wake up coughing. He'd mop his forehead with a handkerchief, look at Levi with his big gray eyes and say, "Come on, Levi, you're going to like your new home," and Levi would narrow his eyes meanly, and turn away, only to be elbowed and needled by his brother Samuel. "Baby," Samuel chided him.

Somewhere along the way on that journey it had come to Levi like a resolution: I don't need anyone. I'm on my own. And then: I shouldn't be Amish, why am I Amish?

Shortly after they moved to Wisconsin, Uncle Enos died. Levi was told that he had cancer, and he had come to Wisconsin to see a special doctor, leaving his wife back home in Missouri. He had planned to return within the month. Now he would never go back and she was unable to make the trip for his funeral. Levi's parents took the buggy to the nearest English neighbor several times to speak to her by telephone.

On the day of the funeral, the driveway that led to his grandparents' house was a solid black line of Amish buggies. This was Levi's first funeral and he noticed everything. Men from the community arrived before dawn to do the farm chores and women took over for his mother, grandma, and sisters. The funeral was held in his grandparents' house and his family sat up close to the open coffin while prayers were said in German and English. The ministers removed their hats first and then every man did the same in unison. Levi tried to focus on anything but the big pine box that held his uncle, as he listened to the ministers talking about death as if it were a living thing. Be prepared to meet death, they said and God has spoken through our brother's death.

After the prayer service they walked single file to a hillside overlooking the farm. Men had dug a big hole and there was a giant pile of dirt. More prayers were said and the coffin was open again. Levi forgot to look away and he saw his uncle all dressed in white with a face of gray stone. After the coffin lid was shut, the coffin was lowered into the hole with ropes, and boards were placed across it before people took turns shoveling dirt on top of it. The shovel would scoop up the dirt with a sound like a whisper and the clump of dirt would hit the coffin with a slap. Whisper-slap, whisper-slap, and the trill of a redwing blackbird answered back. Those were the only sounds Levi heard and just as he thought he might fall asleep, a final prayer was said and everyone walked back to the house.

The kitchen filled up with women and girls and plates of sandwiches. Men grouped in the living room and boys mingled around them. There was a hush of conversation. The house was dense with the smell of coffee and tea and people's sweat. Levi thought about how he would miss his uncle who had always tried to be nice and was seldom serious and stern like most of the other grown-ups. Maybe that was because he didn't feel good and he knew he was going to die.

That November Levi turned five, his mother had a baby named Enos, who had a giant head. His skin was the color of mulberries. Levi's sister Anna told Levi that the baby was extra special because he was different from the rest of them. Levi stared at his baby brother then and noted that he had tiny little eyes and a cry that sounded more like a kitten than a baby boy. He took to peering at the baby's face as the months went by and he got so he could tell whether the baby felt good or bad just by the way his eyebrows arched or frowned and his mouth turned up or down. Sometimes the baby's little mouth would stay open in a hollow Oh! and Levi would stare into the tiny darkness imagining he saw words there all jammed up and trapped behind Enos's tongue.

By this time they had moved out of his grandparents' house into a frame building that would one day be a workshop where his father would build and repair carriages. A foundation was dug for the house, a vast squared-off empty pit that Levi and Samuel liked to slide down into and sometimes had a hard time climbing out. Their mother was so busy with the baby that she didn't scold them much for their dirty clothes and Levi was beginning to like it in Wisconsin, especially when it started snowing. They had the most fun, he and Samuel, pushing chunks of snow into great big mounds so they could climb up and jump off.

In Wisconsin it seemed to snow constantly, and the snow would pile up and drift, forming big canyons all around. One day Levi's parents and siblings went to the barn and told Levi to stay at the house in case the baby woke up, and when the baby did wake up, Levi was to get his mother. He was eager to get out of the house and so he played with little Enos, tickling his tiny hands, cooing at him, touching his soft cheek gently until finally the baby woke up. Levi put on his coat and boots quickly and hurried out to find his mother.

The barn was quite a distance from the house, and walking through the snow was particularly hard because it was so deep, especially for five year-old legs. But for most of the way the snow was frozen solid on top and he could slip along without sinking in. Walking on top of the hard snow was like being on a high-up bridge. Levi could see farther than he'd ever been able to see before, and that made him feel brave and especially strong. He took longer and longer steps, his legs nearly sliding out from under him and he laughed outright at the fun he was having when all of a sudden the snow gave way with a crunch and his feet, legs, body, even his head sank beneath the surface. It happened so fast, he grabbed mightily at the slippery edges as he went down but he couldn't catch himself and the cold wet walls of snow collapsed around him. He was trapped in a snow drift in the dark and encompassing cold. He yelled and screamed until he began to lose his voice. He got so shivery that he curled up into a ball like a cat, tucking his hands in under his neck and his feet together tight and snug. He became very tired and he couldn't feel his hands and feet, and his ears and nose stopped stinging.

    When they eventually found him, he was very still and turning a ghastly shade of blue-white. "We thought you were dead," Samuel told him afterwards. His father had carried him into the house and they pulled off his icy clothing and wrapped him in a blanket. His parents rubbed his hands and feet and dipped them into a bucket of water. At first Levi couldn't feel it and then it stung and tingled so bad he kicked and screamed but he had no voice left, just a croak, and they forcibly held him down as they rubbed him briskly.

    That summer when they returned to Missouri to visit, his Grandpa Levi presented him with a wagon he had made. "I do this for all of my grandsons named Levi," the kind old man said, beaming. The wagon was one of Levi's most prized possessions. Back home in Wisconsin he would use it to haul water to the house and sometimes he'd give his sisters rides in it, pulling them up and over the top of the grassy slopes, letting go of the handle and running alongside with the dogs chasing and barking wildly and his sisters squealing in fear and delight.

    That same summer a big tornado hit their farm. Still without a house, they had settled into the woodshop and made it their home, but it had no basement in which to seek shelter. The children huddled together in a tight circle on the hard kitchen floor with their arms crossed over their heads, the baby at the center wrapped tightly in a blanket, and their parents stooped over them, shielding them as best they could.

The wind got louder and louder outside, roaring into focus over them. At first Levi recognized the sounds of leaves blowing and branches snapping, of acorns hitting the roof. Soon it was like nothing in the world he'd ever heard, a bellowing and high whistle so loud they closed their eyes and covered their ears. The windows blew out suddenly and shards of glass rained around them. His sisters were sobbing, and over the deafening howling outside, the wailing and thrashing, crashing and thudding as things hit the house, the ripping, tearing and tumbling that filled his ears, Levi could hear the horses screaming in the barn.

When it was quiet outside, quite suddenly silent, not even a fluttering breeze or birdsong, their parents stumbled to their feet and the children followed. The baby was crying hoarsely, maybe he had been the whole time, but they had not heard. Their father picked him up and held him tight and gave thanks that no one was hurt. Levi looked around. Glass, dirt and leaves covered the floor. The sun shone in where slats of wood had been torn away, casting tall narrow beams of eerie light onto the filthy trash-strewn floor. They all got to work cleaning up. Levi's mother went into the kitchen to get the broom, and all along the way she would bend down to pick something up and make strange bird-like noises. She rescued dishes and pans and utensils from the floor and put them on the table. The tabletop was soon heaped with mismatched and desultory items.

When the mess was somewhat contained inside, they wrenched open the door and went outside and looked about them in astonishment. They hardly recognized their surroundings. It was difficult to get around. One tree had toppled in the yard, and another had split, blocking the drive. Limbs and leaves and splintered wood were all over the place. They stepped away from the woodshop to survey the damage and saw a large piece of the roof pointing at the sky like a broken wing. Lose boards were still attached, but dangled dangerously overhead. The clothesline that had been held up by two sturdy t-poles was up in the oak tree, clothes and poles and all, towels and dresses and shirts dangling from the rope that wrapped the branches like colored lights that Levi had once seen on an English house at Christmas.

They made their way down to the barn and just stood there and stared. The barn, which wasn't fully built yet, bulged at the sides, as if something was trying to push itself out. Inside horses were neighing and cows were mooing and groaning. There were thumps and bangs and rumbling. "I have to get the animals out," Levi's father said. "Katie, open the field gate." His mother handed the baby to his oldest sister, Lizzie, and struggled to open the bent and twisted corral gate. "It's unusable," his father said, so his parents climbed over the fence. His father entered the barn cautiously, while his mother hurried over to the barbed wire field gate and propped it open. In moments, their father struggled to lead the first frightened horse out of the barn. His own buggy horse, usually obedient, reared and struck out with her high front legs, her eyes rolling. He'd yank her down and she'd fling her head up trying to get free.

His mother, in her haste to get out of the corral, got tangled in some wire fencing that had blown in and she went down hard, but she was up in seconds and back over the fence. Her teary face was streaked with blood and dirt. As soon as his mother was out of the corral his father got the halter off the buggy horse and the mare took off at a gallop, careening through the gate. In her haste, her legs flew out from under her and she fell flat on her side and slid into the fence with a thud. But she scrambled to her feet and ran into the field and she didn't stop until she was nearly out of sight at the far fence.

The second horse refused to lead. She planted her hooves in the barn doorway, Levi's father pulled and commanded and slapped the rope against her side and she jerked away again and again. Finally, he grabbed a piece of wood that was lying there and waved it behind her as he unhooked her halter, and smacked her on the butt. She scooted out into the corral and veered off to the far corner, her eyes wide and crazed. The percherons were brought out two at a time and they joined the stubborn standardbred on the far side of the corral. Then the cows were pushed out, and they milled around near the horses, causing the horses to dance about calling to each other and bumping into one another while the cows clumped together in a big sorry mass, all the animals raising an uproar.

The bull came last led by the nose. In unspoken signals, Levi's mother tossed a bale of hay down to keep the horses and cows away from the barn door and field gate, while Levi's father led the bull all the way out into the field and unhooked the chain. The bull stood still as a statue as Levi's father hustled back through the corral, darted over to the horses and cows, snatched up what was left of the hay and tossed it over the fence out of their reach into the field. Then he slapped the lead draft horse on the butt and commanded him to: "Go on, get," as he jumped up on the fence to safety. The horses followed the leader through the gate out into the field, but stopped short at the sight of the massive bull.

Levi's father ran over to the fence line nearest to the bull and yelled and clapped his hands. The bull trotted off bellowing, the horses took off in unison running across the field to the farthest corner with the first horse, and the cows pushed through the gateway into the field in a disheveled mob.

It was only then that Levi became aware of his little baby brother's sad, sorry whimpering which must have been going on throughout. They made their way back and his mother and Lizzie took little Enos inside while everyone else began to pick up what they could, branches, rope, a broken piece of board. They looked to their father. He chose a particularly large downed tree limb and hauled it behind him toward the big hole in the ground that was dug for the house foundation. "We're out of money now anyway," he said to himself, and to the children: "Drag what you can over to this pit and push it over the edge."

Samuel and Edna carried a piece of roofing together and swung their arms out one, two, three, letting it go into the open pit with a crash. Their father nodded his approval and told them he was going to check on Grandpa Samuel and Grandma Edna.

At first it bothered Levi that they were filling in the hole, for he had been curious to know just exactly how they would build a house on top of it, but soon he enjoyed scavenging sizeable chunks of wood and pitching them high over the open pit. The heavy unwieldy pieces had to be dragged over to the edge, and that was hard work, but it was satisfying to shove them, sometimes sitting on the ground and using both feet to get them over the ledge.

When their father returned that evening, he reported that their grandparents had lost their barn roof and silo top, but that was the worst of it. Then he hitched up the buggy because their mother wanted to take little Enos to the hospital. Levi stood with his sister, Anna, and watched the buggy carry away his parents and his baby brother. Anna said, "At eight months you weren't just crawling, Levi, you were pulling yourself up onto anything you could reach and trying to walk. We had to watch you all the time!" She gave him a little hug and he thought about his baby brother who couldn't even hold his head up and had never sat up or crawled but just waved his arms and legs in small jerky circles.

The rest of the summer was spent re-building. When Levi asked about the house that was supposed to go on top of the hole in the ground he never did get a real answer and yet that hole never was filled in. It stood there off to the side like a promise of what might be and during dry season it was a vast dirt pit that he and his brother could slide down into getting their clothes filthy for which they'd sometimes be swatted, and when it rained the pit became a huge brown muddy pond for chucking rocks into, or throwing sticks for the dogs. He could recall his mother asking, pleading and commanding that they stay away from the foundation, but how could they? It was too enticing and they were just boys.

As the years went by, Levi's family built a new wood shop, a pump house, a big dairy barn and two machine sheds. There was also a chicken coop, a wash shed, and much later, when Anna grew up and got married, a second house just like the first one, for Levi's parents had made what had originally been intended to be the workshop into a fine home.

An enclosed porch led to the kitchen, which had a cook stove at the center with a counter on one side and a hutch opposite. They ate at a big table with a bench along the wall and a chair at either end, two or three chairs across from the bench. They'd set food to cool on the porch windowsill since there was no refrigeration and water had to be carried up from the pump house by the bucket. The living room was on the other side of the kitchen chimney with a woodstove for heat, a utility closet, a desk and chair, a couch. The house had lots of natural light, windows all around and they used oil lamps or Coleman gas lanterns after dark.

Upstairs there were two bedrooms, boys on one side and girls on the other. Siblings slept together in double beds. The Amish can't have beds any bigger than double or full size. Later, Levi's parents would add a bedroom for themselves on the first floor and a basement underneath for canning.

At the age of six, Amish children start having regular chores and they begin school. Levi and his brother Samuel would get up every day at 4:30 in the morning. "The first few years until I was old enough to milk," Levi says, "I would feed and water the calves and cows, and sweep the barn floor. Anything I was physically able to do I was doing." Another chore was weeding the garden. Levi's mother had very large garden where she grew carrots, peas, green beans, navy beans, corn, strawberries, raspberries, cucumbers, potatoes, tomatoes, and rhubarb for jams and pies. She had flowers everywhere, too. "We'd be on our hands and knees in the garden all summer long," Levi recalls. His sisters' chores included carrying firewood.

Breakfast had always been Levi's favorite meal, perhaps because when they fasted for Amish holy days it was only breakfast that they had to skip. Breakfast was usually served around seven, and it typically consisted of tomatoes in gravy on sliced bread or biscuits with eggs and sausage. Then they always had cereal after, hot cereal called Farina, similar to Cream of Wheat.

They had to be at school on time and they didn't want to be tardy or they'd get the sharp stick reprimand, so at 8:45 or so Levi's mother or one of his sisters would come out to the barn to call for them, and they'd tear into the house to clean up, change clothes and run to school. It was about a quarter-mile away and they hurried. Punishment for tardiness was something to be avoided, it not only hurt, but it was very embarrassing to be hit on your backside by the teacher right there in front of everybody.

The schoolhouse was on his grandparents' farm about a ten-minute walk from Levi's house. The main schoolroom had three windows on each side, a woodstove at the back, and a rear door that was never used for some reason they could never fathom. Thirty desks for grades one through eight faced the lone teacher's desk, which stood immediately to the right of the front entrance. Two big blackboards were on either side of the room and bookshelves with about two hundred books filled the back corner.

Class was from 9:00 until 3:30. Everyone learned together, the teacher would hand out class assignments first thing, and then walk around the desks helping where it was needed. There was a morning recess at 9:30 for about fifteen minutes, a break at lunch, then a half hour recess until quarter to one or one o'clock when the teacher would read aloud from Laura Ingalls or the Hardy

Boys, only "child-friendly" series, nothing like Louis L'Amour, whose adventure westerns Levi discovered and enjoyed after he left the Amish.

At two o'clock there was another fifteen-minute recess when the boys would play what is commonly thought of as baseball, but they called it dare base. They played other games like Andy on, hide and seek, dodge ball, and, of course, the universal game of tag in good weather. In winter, they'd carve out snow blocks with a handsaw and make snow houses.

"We'd go out into snowdrifts, cut snow into blocks, and set them down for walls, stuffing the cracks with soft snow," Levi explains. "The roof was plywood weighted down with fire wood. We'd go inside our snow houses and talk or read. We read a lot as kids. School went till 8th grade when we were fourteen."

The quality of their education reflected the fact that the teachers only went through 8th grade, too, but the curriculum was strict. "We all spoke Amish (Pennsylvania Dutch) at home," Levi says.

Some of the more common Amish words are: gut (good), yah (yes), neh (no), esa (eat!), Gott (God), shlofa (sleep), galas (suspenders), stroh hoots (straw hats), hingleflesh (fried or broasted chicken), and grumbatta mush (mashed potatoes).

"Monday through Thursday we were required to speak English even on the playground. On Friday everything was in German. We had a German textbook and we read the Old Testament in German as well. We seldom had any homework. If a subject was hard, like fractions, I might ask my father for help after dinner," Levi recalls.

The Amish celebrate Thanksgiving, the day after Thanksgiving, Christmas, the day after Christmas, New Years, Old Christmas (January 6), Good Friday, and Easter. On holy days they would fast at breakfast and then spend the rest of the day driving their buggies from farm to farm, family to family. "There was no work on holy days except morning chores. We would go and visit and have a big lunch," Levi says.

Christmas presents are given at school. Each child would draw one name of another child. The presents were usually ordered from a catalogue. They would get things like gloves, flashlights, scarves, games, and puzzles. To celebrate at school, they'd sing hymns. After school, friends and neighbors would gather in their homes to visit and the children would play. Summer break began in mid-to-late April, and they'd start back to school in September.

During those first few years in Wisconsin, home life was difficult because Levi's baby brother Enos was sick so much of the time. Levi would try to make him smile by talking silly to him and doing a jig. He did this because he knew it made his mother happy to see him playing with the baby (they still called Enos the baby even though he was nearly two), but sometimes it didn't matter what Levi did, Enos was miserable. He'd be strapped in the baby seat or the wind-up swing and his little eyebrows would scrunch together and his mouth would bunch up and Levi would feel so sad just to look at him. Not understanding made it worse.

When Levi was in the second grade, Enos caught pneumonia and died. The house filled up just as his grandmother's house had filled up when Uncle Enos died, and there were plates and plates of food and coffee and tea. Levi overheard so many people lamenting that the poor boy was just two and a half years-old and he had never walked or talked. Levi's mother cried softly by herself for days and Levi began to think, life is so bleak, I'm going to kill myself. I'm going to stop eating. He gave away his treasures to his sisters and brothers. His sisters were given pictures he had saved from a calendar. His brother got some rocks and a wooden spinning top.

Nobody even noticed, and Levi didn't die, of course. It turned out he was unable to stop eating. It couldn't be done. Whether he truly wished to die or was expressing a young boy's grief or cry for attention is anybody's guess.

When he was eight or nine, Levi started milking with Samuel. They milked ten to twelve Holsteins by hand and the boys also had to deal with the bull. "We had to be careful with the bull, neither one of us was ever hurt but we'd known other Amish who had been gored by a bull," Levi recalls.

All farm work was done by hand with draft horses pulling the plow and disc, and dragging the harrow. All clothes were handmade by Levi's mother and when they were twelve or so, his sisters began to learn how to sew clothes. The males wore simple shirts with no collars, denim pants with buttoned waists, plain shoes from a catalogue, and bowl-style haircuts. The girls wore plain dresses with aprons, and a covering on their heads. Their hair was as long as it would grow and always pinned up and covered with a prayer cap and sometimes a bonnet over that.

Every other Sunday Levi and his siblings did not have to attend church—but their father, who was a minister, certainly did, and their mother went with him. Those Sundays were called In Between Sundays and they were like little vacations to Levi. Sure he had to do his chores but after that he was free because his parents would go off to church in the morning and be gone the entire day.

One of his favorite activities on In Between Sundays was teasing his sisters. They'd be playing house with their dolls and he'd spy on them and mock them, or run up and snatch a doll and roar away giggling. They'd chase after him and he'd race off to hide the doll somewhere in the house, or tear outside and toss the doll high up into a tree or sling it deep beneath a dark brier-infested bush.

"Get it for me, get it for me," one of his sisters would cry and the others would say, "We're going to tell, Levi." Usually after awhile, he'd climb the tree and toss the doll down or slink under the bush and bring it out, brushing it off, but sometimes he'd lose interest in what he thought of as a game and the doll would be forgotten. Whether his sisters found the doll or not, they never enjoyed the game and they always told on him when their parents got home.

This occurred almost every In Between Sunday and when his parents returned from church he knew they'd go into the house and hear about what he'd done and his mother or father would come out to find him busily doing his chores and the first few times he got just a talking-to. On the next In Between Sunday they'd warn him as they were leaving, "Levi, don't tease your sisters," and when they returned and were told what he'd done, he'd get the switch, which usually meant up to five hits with a fly-swatter. Knowing he'd be punished didn't cure him of the teasing bug, though, since it was like a sport to him and they were his sisters after all.

When he was ten or eleven, Levi was in the barn cleaning out the stalls when his parents came home from church. He and Samuel had already done the milking and turned the cows and horses out. They hadn't released the bull yet, and he was still chained to the post by the ring in his nose. Samuel unhitched the buggy horse, their parents went into the house, and Levi continued cleaning out the barn.

The two brothers had spent most of the afternoon fishing in the creek and it had been hours since Levi had stolen Edna's baby doll and flung it under the porch out of her view. Yet when his father strode out of the house, marched straight to the barn, and stopped in the doorway to select a two-by-four from a stack of wood that was lying there, Levi's back stiffened up and he propped the shovel against the stall rail. He knew what was coming.

"Levi, didn't your mother and I tell you not to tease your sisters? Where is Edna's doll?" His father's mouth was set in a thin solemn line.

Levi looked at the two-by-four in his father's left hand and his eyes darted to the barn doorway. The late afternoon sun streamed in like an invitation. "It's under the porch. I'll get it," he said eagerly. He understood there'd be no escaping what was coming to him, but he was a firm believer in giving it a try. He strode down the aisle and made an attempt to bypass his father. His sisters, Edna and Anna, peered down from a spot just behind the lilac bush. "I'm sorry," he called out.

"Go inside," their father said over his shoulder as he caught Levi by the arm. The girls ran into the house. The grip on Levi's shoulder tightened. His father forced him to turn around and bend over and the first thwack was so swift and hard that it knocked the wind out of him. Levi fell to his knees. His face was mere inches from a mound of dung on which a beautiful blue and black butterfly alighted. He focused on the butterfly, clenched his jaw, clamped his lips and teeth together stubbornly, furiously, and then he jumped back up.

He braced himself as four more whacks came in quick succession. He couldn't help it, he yelled out his outrage and pain. His voice carried up to the house where his mother and sisters were preparing supper, and over to the field where the horses were grazing. The clatter of pots and pans from the house seemed to increase with every shout. The horses whinnied back and forth as if to say, are we safe here? The bull huffed and pawed the ground but he did not try to break away, as the chain was still attached to the ring in his incredibly sensitive nose. Samuel was nowhere to be seen.

The two-by-four was dropped back on the pile with a thud and his father left. Levi held his arms straight down at his sides as his hands made tight fists. His backside burned. Roiling pain wrapped around him like a blanket. His father's heavy feet trudged across the dirt and gravel onto the grass, and moments later, stepped up onto the porch. The screen door creaked open and banged shut. Only then did Levi turn around. Edna was at the kitchen window clutching her doll.

He went back to shoveling out the stalls and every single movement made him suck in his breath with a gasp. He didn't stop feeling sore for days. It hurt to put on or take off his clothes, and he wanted to cry those first few times he forgot and sat down too hard. Later that week when he and Samuel and some other boys went skinny-dipping at the creek Levi kept his backside hidden from view. He was embarrassed for anyone to see the bruises his father had left on him with the two-by-four.

Seven

Levi was happy to be done with school at fifteen, since Amish only go through the eighth grade. He worked full time on the farm, at a local sawmill and in his father's woodworking shop making crafts for a specialty store in Augusta called "The Woodshed." He would cut jack-o-lantern faces out of a patterned board with a jigsaw and sometimes paint them. Though the Amish don't celebrate Halloween, they call it Satan's holiday, they will make Halloween crafts for money. They were paid by the piece and all the money Levi made during the day went to his parents but anything he made after chores and supper was his money to keep.

At seventeen, when Levi got his own horse and buggy, he began dating Rosanna. Amish encourage matching up—for instance it's a custom at wedding suppers for young people to sit in couples and if a boy doesn't pair up with a girl of his own choosing, one will be chosen for him. Levi and Rosanna had known each other since the 5th grade when she had moved to the community. She was pretty and shy, different from his sisters and other girls at school, and he found that appealing. They sat together at his cousin's wedding supper when they were thirteen, and they'd been sitting together ever since. After the Sunday night hymn sings, he'd escort Rosanna back to her house, sometimes alone, sometimes with another couple, and they'd play games and talk and kiss.

The following spring when Levi started studying to be baptized so he could join the church, he began courting Rosanna in earnest, not just on date night but on other nights as well—standing in her front yard, shining his flashlight on her window after the old folks had gone to bed. She'd meet him at the front door and they'd go inside, he'd settle in the courtship rocker and take her on his lap and they'd hold each other and kiss until the early hours of the morning.

Like every other Saturday and every day for that matter, Levi had chores around the farm. One of them was leading the two buggy horses out to the field behind the barn, a chore he had done so many times he could do it in his sleep. He stopped the horses at the gate, a single strand of barbed wire. As was his custom, he unhooked the wire and laid it flat in the grass so the horses could step over it.

Barbed wire was like a dangerous snake to man and animal if not handled right. It was almost a living thing. That was the very reason that he and his brother Samuel were supposed to use care and pull the strand of barbed wire all the way back and hook it onto the fence post before leading the horses through the opening. Accidents are made of carelessness, a stubborn instinct to cut corners and a bit of laziness. Dropping the barbed wire to the ground was a simple shortcut they had taken many times before and nothing had ever gone wrong. The horses easily cleared the strand of barbed wire, just as the first horse did on that day.

Levi led her into the open field, unhooked her rope and slapped her butt to make her move out of the way. He watched as she trotted a few yards over to the left and waited for her stable mate. Then he proceeded to do the same with the second mare, tugging gently on the lead, easing her along.

Or was he impatient that day? He had so many jobs lined up already, cleaning out the milk cans, painting the porch, building a pump house, shoring up the corncrib. He may have yanked on her halter. And looking back he thought it was possible that he hadn't been paying much attention and he had let the barbed wire fall a bit haphazardly onto the humps of fescue where it could snag a hoof, tighten around an ankle, and trip up even the most agile animal.

He always watched to make sure the horses' hooves cleared the barbed wire and so he saw the thorny wire pop up like a snare when the second mare's back left foot nicked it. The horse kicked back instinctively causing the barbed wire to dig in and puncture her skin. In a frenzy of fear she lunged forward. Levi held on tight to her halter and leaned down at an awkward angle in an attempt to untangle the wire and free her leg. He tried to calm her, saying, "Easy, easy," in a soothing voice, but all she seemed to sense was his growing alarm.

Levi had been dealing with horses and cows since he was a little boy, and he generally had no fear, but as he reached for the tightening strand of barbed wire, still holding onto her halter, he felt her muscles tense up suddenly. The mare had suddenly had enough and she leapt forward. The halter was ripped from his hand, the fence post was torn from the earth and Levi was flung hard to his side, his thigh bearing most of the force. He heard a gut wrenching snap and searing pain shot from his knee and up to his hip like a lightning bolt. "Dad!" he shouted, as he held his injured leg aloft. Even the slightest movement or pressure made him dizzy. His panicked eyes searched around for someone, anyone, but all he saw were the two mares thundering away, leaving in their wake the uprooted fence post and a good portion of the barbed wire fence.

Much of what happened next was described to him later, but as the pain ebbed and flowed with his consciousness, he was aware of being lifted up onto his father's shoulder and carried fireman-style through the barnyard, across the grass toward the shade of the large oak tree where at their mother's direction, his brothers and sisters had dragged the dark blue couch from the living room. His father ran off, his sister patted his forehead with a damp cloth, and his mother held his hand as she said over and over, "Your father has gone to call the taxi."

While some Amish have telephones for their businesses, Levi's community did not. If they needed to call someone they went to the nearest non-Amish neighbor or to the phone shed at the taxi driver's house. The man they referred to as "the taxi" hired out exclusively to the Amish. He was the one they called when a horse and buggy wouldn't do and Levi's parents had realized quickly that they couldn't fit Levi into a buggy without causing him tremendous pain. While they would certainly go to the hospital for situations such as this, they would never call for an ambulance. Their faith required as much self-sufficiency as possible.

After awhile the horrible throbbing faded away and Levi's leg became numb, his mind grew foggy, and he wondered where the pain had gone. He started shivering and shaking. His teeth were chattering as a quilt came down heavy on top of him, reminding his body of the pain. His father rubbed his arms. His sister offered him water. There was moaning and darkness all around him like the coming of a thunder storm. The sounds issuing from him were alien and animal-like and his mother's anxious eyes searched his for signs of recognition.

When the taxi driver arrived, he peered down at Levi on the sofa under the tree with the family gathered tightly around and a shadow flickered across his face as he glanced at Levi's leg. He started backing away. "There's no point in taking him to the hospital. It's Saturday. The hospital's closed."

They didn't question the taxi driver, if he said the hospital was closed on Saturday then it must be so. But of course it was not closed, the driver simply did not want to take Levi to the hospital. Perhaps he was shocked by the sight of the severely broken leg, and worried about being held responsible even though it is a well-known fact that the Amish do not participate in lawsuits. Or his lie could have stemmed from his aversion to having to help load the young man in the car. At any rate there was the sound of a car door slam and a motor starting.

Levi slept, waking every so often to see the blue shards of sky through the tree branches, the leaves like handkerchiefs waving, worried faces looking down on him, his mother, his father, his sisters and brothers, all in a blur of shadows. A cup of water was pressed to his mouth and he choked. The water spewed out as a cough ripped through his throat like a quake, knocking the cup over on his chest. The quilt was even heavier with the dampness, pressing down on his body. He must have grimaced and groaned some more, because it was pulled off of him and his mother was there with his sister, Edna.

"Edna, hold my arm steady," his mother said. "Levi, I'm going to have to cut the side seam of your pants. Your leg is puffing up and..." She didn't finish. He felt the scissors gliding along his leg and the tug of the denim as she held the fabric taunt; fear rose inside him as the scissors inched closer to his knee. He clamped his hand on his mother's arm to stop her but she kept cutting as she said softly, "I'm sorry," over and over again. When she was done, she folded the fabric back to expose his leg and her eyes widened. His leg was a bulging blur of blood and skin with a jagged bone pushing out the side. It was all so completely misshapen it didn't appear to be a part of him nor a human limb at all, but it throbbed and burned and even seemed to have a pulse as it rose and fell against the newly cut denim. A mighty surge of nausea caused him to vomit and gag before dropping back onto the couch into a dizzying sleep.

Time passed but the pain did not. By late afternoon a car pulled in the drive and the man they called the chiropractor walked over to the sofa and gazed for a long time at Levi's leg without touching it. After awhile he said solemnly, "It's very swollen. Looks like a bad sprain. Ice it to try and keep the swelling down, and tell him to hold still."

Before nightfall Levi and the couch were carried inside. The pain ebbed and flowed like tidal waves. The ice melted quickly in the summer heat and the weight of the soggy rag against his bare skin made his leg ache deep inside. It was unbearable. After everyone else went to bed, the pain became so persistent that he had to bury his head in the side of the couch to muffle the low moans emanating from his mouth. He prayed dear Lord make this pain go away, dear Lord make this pain go away, dear Lord make this pain go away, a mantra to unsuccessfully try to keep the pain at bay. By Sunday he was eating some. By Monday he was trying to get around by holding onto chairs, walls, and doorways, making his way from here to there, dragging the log of a leg behind him. The rags they used as bandages had to be replaced almost every hour at first, and then only once or twice a day.

Levi could not bear to be idle and he was going to get his life back if by sheer will. He tried ignoring the pain, and he grew to hate it so much that suppressing it made him feel stronger. Going to the outhouse was pure misery, though, because he insisted on making that trip alone, hopping, stumbling and falling, taking the one step up, turning around adjusting his pants over the swollen appendage, sitting down awkwardly on the sharp plain wood. Afterwards there was an intense ache that throbbed deep in his bone causing the skin on his leg to turn red and burn to the touch.

He thought of others who had it so much worse, his little brother Enos who had died so young, only two. He had never walked or talked. Or his Uncle Enos who had lived into his twenties, but was sick so much of the time that he finally just died. Levi had a bad leg. It would get better. He would make sure it got better. He was getting married soon. He refused to be a weak crippled husband who limped about always needing help.

Wednesday his father brought in crutches he had borrowed from Jacob Miller who had broken his ankle when he fell from a barn roof. Levi took to them immediately. After a week, his underarms stung and were rubbed raw where the crutches pressed in, so his mother folded up rags and tucked them inside his shirt for padding and it was okay. Whenever he could get by without the crutches he would, half-hopping, half-limping.

The chiropractor came around a couple of times after that to stare at Levi's thigh. It had gone from black, purple and green, to yellow and dull brown. Skin was growing over the protruding bone but it didn't look right and it was hot to the touch. The leg itself was crooked and it bulged on one side but the swelling had gone down and the pain had become less noticeable, hurting most at the end of the day. One afternoon the chiropractor said to Levi's father, "Looks like he may need to have an x-ray."

They took the buggy to town and Levi hobbled into the doctor's office. When the doctor saw him he said sternly, "Young man, you have a broken leg. Get off of it!" His father helped him up onto the white sheeted cot in the x-ray room. A heavy blanket was thrown over him and his father was told to wait in the hall. A young woman close to his own age introduced herself as a technician as she reached for his leg and stretched it out. He sucked in his breath, and his eyes opened wide. "I'm so sorry," she said. "I've got to position you for the film." She handled him more gently after that, warning him before she touched him, explaining as she manually turned him this way and that. When she was satisfied with his position she'd tell him to lie still and hold his breath before stepping behind a wall to hit the switch. The machine would zoom in on him and start cranking. When it stopped, she'd come out from behind the wall and gently turn him on his hip, place his arms over his head, exposing first one side, and then the other. Every manipulation was painful and sent shooting pains through him, but after the first time he was silent. He just gritted his teeth.

He was led into an office where his father sat waiting. The doctor was about his father's age but surly, snappish, and irritated. He studied one large black sheet of film after another and then spoke directly to Levi's father. "He has a severe fracture in the femur just above the knee. He needs surgery right away. We'll have to break the bone and re-set it with screws." He never once looked at Levi's face and when he spoke to Levi's father he used an accusatory tone.

"How much will surgery cost?" Joe asked.

The doctor glared at him. "My receptionist can tell you." The doctor was dismissive, his tone impatient. He walked out of the office so abruptly, they expected him to return. After awhile Levi and his father left also. They went to stand by the reception desk which was shut off from the waiting room by a glass panel. They stood there for a very long time and finally a young woman deigned to slide open the glass. "That will be a three hundred and forty dollars, cash, cashier's check or money order."

Levi's father counted out the cash and slid it across the counter as he asked, "How much will the surgery cost?"

"Hold on." The glass slid shut and they watched her disappear from view. Another ten minutes passed before she returned. The panel was opened slightly. "Surgery will be in the range of ten to twelve thousand dollars. When would you like us to schedule it? He has Thursday at six a.m. or next Tuesday at eleven a.m."

Joe asked for a phone number so they could call, then they left the doctor's office, climbed into the buggy, and headed home. When they got to their own drive his father turned to him and asked quietly, "Do you want surgery or do you want to be a cripple for the rest of your life?"

Levi said, "I want surgery." He knew his father would have to borrow money from the Amish but he didn't worry about it. It wasn't that he didn't care, simply that he didn't want to be a cripple for the rest of his life.

Thursday morning they left home in pre-dawn darkness and drove the buggy to the hospital where Levi was instructed to take off all his clothes and put on a flimsy little shirt that barely came to his knees. He was unbearably embarrassed, but did what he was told. The last thing he remembered was lying on a small bed as he was wheeled down a narrow hall, the ceiling panels and florescent lights coasting by looking almost like a checker board. A woman in a face-mask asked him to count backwards from one hundred, and then he woke up and was intensely sick. He opened his eyes, closed them again, and groaned. His father was there on the periphery of his vision and also a nurse. His leg felt wooden, not a part of him. The dull ache in his thigh that he'd grown accustomed to was gone to be replaced by the worst headache and stomachache he had ever had.

"Levi," the nurse said loudly. "How are you feeling?"
"Not so good."
"Are you sick to your stomach?"
"Yes."

She placed a metal pan by his side. "Use this if you need to up-chuck. You were in surgery for four and a half hours. The doctor opened up your leg and reset the bone with a metal plate and seven screws." Levi's leg began to throb as if in response. "You're sick from the anesthesia I suspect," the nurse said. "That happens. You'll have stay here until the nausea subsides." She made a notation on his chart and left the room. Levi felt his father's hand on his arm and then something happened to the rest of the day and he didn't recall a thing.

The next morning the surgeon came into Levi's hospital room and stood at the end of his bed. He was wearing a bright yellow short-sleeved shirt and plaid pants. Levi blinked a few times trying to clear his vision. The surgeon picked up the clipboard that was hanging there and marked it with a pen. Then he peeled back the sheet that covered Levi and asked, "How're you doing? I'm going to have to remove the drain tube." Without waiting for a response the doctor ripped the bandage off and wrenched and tugged and tore something out of Levi's thigh. The burning searing pain was so excruciating that Levi yelled and threw himself backwards, banging his head on the wall behind the bed. He glimpsed the seven-inch long bloody tube as the doctor dropped it into a pan.

"We'll have to remove the metal plate in about a year. But I think you'll be able to do most of what you did before." The doctor's tone was matter-of-fact. He was not sympathetic and he didn't apologize for obviously causing Levi undue pain. He simply turned his sharp squint on Levi for an instant and then the nurse took his place. She cleaned the wound and replaced the bandage. She wasn't particularly careful or kind either, as if she thought, as the doctor did, that Levi was too stupid to merit their concern.

Levi was in the hospital for three days total, and twice he risked turning on the television but was so afraid the nurses would tell his parents he was watching TV that he turned it off again quickly. Mostly he lay in bed and went over again and again the moment when the horse banged into him and knocked him to the ground. The point of impact when he realized in a split instant of excruciating agony that nothing would be the same again. He was furious with himself for placing the barbed wire in the grass instead of hooking it up to the post. One careless attempt to save time had cost him dearly--the incredible inconvenience of the past weeks trying to get around with a broken leg, and now this, the humiliating hospital with its haughty nurses and that doctor with his narrow eyes, rough treatment, and disregard. Levi couldn't help thinking it was because he was Amish that they had treated him that way and for perhaps the hundredth time in his life he thought, I shouldn't be Amish.

His parents paid the hospital bill with twelve thousand dollars they borrowed from an Amish man in the community, and Levi went home with a leg brace, which he removed as many times a day as he could so that he could stretch and work his leg. He was determined to get better as soon as possible and to do most everything he had done before, as the doctor had promised. A month later when he got married, he left the leg brace in his old bedroom. The metal plate and seven screws would not be removed for another seven years.

November and December are wedding months for the Amish. After Levi and Rosanna were attendants for two of his buddies, he asked her, "Do you think we should get married?" She agreed happily, both of their parents concurred, and Levi went to the deacon the next Sunday to ask permission to marry, a formality—the deacon refers the request to the ministers and the wedding is published (announced) at the service. The groom personally invites his relatives and friends (distant relatives are invited by letter).

As was the custom, Levi stayed over at Rosanna's parents' house the day before to help build the tables for the reception. At dawn he and Rosanna and their attending couples went to the neighbors' house where the three-hour ceremony was held. Then back to Rosanna's house for the reception which lasted until midnight. Tables were laden with roasts, mashed potatoes, salads, bowls of fruit, pies and puddings. Presents were piled on the bed—new pots and pans, dishes, utensils, tablecloths, towels. There were games, singing, and much joyful visiting, and then he drove her home, to their own house, the house his parents had given them.

Lying beside Rosanna in the new double bed that had been a gift from her parents, holding her in his arms for the very first time, Levi was happy. He didn't think about the future or the past, just that moment there with Rosanna, as man and wife, how soft her skin was, how sweet she smelled, how fulfilled he felt.

Eight
Augusta, Wisconsin 1996
"Levi's Back"

November and December were agonizing for Rosanna. Everything was as it had been before Levi left, except for the way she felt. She was tense, afraid, and suspicious of every fleeting glance or flicker from the corner of her eye. She kept waiting for a sign that Levi was preparing to leave again. They had resumed their lives as best they could but Levi could not recommit to the church until his hair grew out, and that seemed to hold him apart from Rosanna. He was remote and distant, often lost in thought, even when they lay together at night, he would touch her the way he used to but it was almost like the touch of a stranger and he would say things like, "We really won't be able to make a go of this until we move off my parents' farm."

"But how can we do that, Levi? Where would we go?"

"We'll borrow money and buy our own place."

Rosanna liked that idea, but she still had doubts about Levi. One day they were eating lunch at Levi's parents' house when a mineral salesman came by. Levi went to the door—he said he knew the man, his name was Lester Phillips, and he was a member of the church Levi had attended with the logger. When the two men stepped out onto the porch to chat, everyone at the table strained to hear what they were saying. The man asked how Levi was doing, and Levi said he was all right.

"Joe," Katie whispered urgently. "Go out there and interrupt." Joe refused with a firm shake of the head. They were scared to death for Levi. In their way of seeing, it was a bad conversation; the man was an outsider and therefore evil. "Please go out there Joe and get Levi to come back inside."

"No," Joe said.

They heard Mr. Phillips preparing to leave. "Well Levi," he said. "If you'd ever like to talk it over, if you change your mind don't be afraid to call me." The door was shut and Levi returned to the table. The meal was finished in silence.

That night as they were getting ready for bed Rosanna said, "You're not going to leave again."

Levi said, "I don't know, not yet at least."

"Okay, then I'm going to leave, too," she told him and a shiver went up her spine. She wasn't sure she meant it, she didn't know if she really had the courage to do it, but making such a promise felt right. She didn't want him to go without her that much she knew, yet it was almost as if she felt that she should watch him constantly so that she'd have a warning, an opportunity to change her mind. That kind of vigilance was impossible, though, since Levi was gone before daylight and she left for school at eight.

Even if she was always home before five, Levi sometimes didn't show up for dinner. He ate wherever he happened to be, whether he was working out for other Amish, helping at frolics, in town with his father, or even right next door at his parents' house, knowing she was home, that as his wife, she wanted to prepare his evening meal. She tried not to fret about it or dwell on the thought that if she could only get pregnant, absolutely everything would be different.

Levi had seemed to fall back into the rhythm of the farm with ease and resolve—milking at 4:30 a.m., tending livestock, fixing fences, taking the buggy to town to pick up supplies with his father. She could hear the two men, father and son, sawing and hammering Saturday afternoons away in the woodshop, making crafts for The Woodshed as if there had never been a terrible breach between them.

By early January their days and nights had taken on a familiarity of routine, yet Rosanna still didn't know if she would go with Levi if he decided to leave again, so she tried not to think about it. School kept her busy Monday through Friday, evenings and weekends were filled with family and friends, quilting bees and singings. Levi's buddies had several children by then and he didn't say anything to her but she knew he had to be thinking that in the two and a half years they'd been married, they had relations often, particularly since his return in October and still no pregnancy. Rosanna was beginning to give up hope that she would ever have a child with Levi. It could be her punishment for befriending Eva, for confronting Eva's mother and forcing the woman to acknowledge what had been going on between Eva and her brother. But more than likely the reason she couldn't conceive was because Levi had left the Amish once, and he intended to do so again. His punishment would also be her punishment.

One frigid Friday night toward the end of January Levi was already in bed when Rosanna came home from making pies and cakes at Katie's for a frolic the next day. She climbed the stairs wearily, undressed, pulled on her nightgown, and got into bed, turning on her side to face away from him even though he was so quiet she knew he was still awake. She truly hoped he wouldn't reach for her; she just wanted to go to sleep. She was finally dozing off when he spoke and what he said woke her up completely.

"Tomorrow I'll go to the neighbor's and call Bob. Doug and Ellen sent all of my stuff there in case anybody asks. I'll tell him, I want to leave but not yet. I need driving lessons."

"All right." Rosanna sat up, pulling the blankets around her shoulders. So now it begins, she thought, and she fell asleep sitting in an upright position. When she woke up the sun was streaming across the bed, Levi's side was empty, of course, and she rubbed her sore neck remembering what he had told her the night before. She did not feel so much apprehensive, as excited. It had begun, and he had included her in the plan. That was the only thing that mattered.

On the following Saturday, Rosanna and Levi took the horse and buggy to Bob's house about ten miles away and they were welcomed inside by Bob's wife, Laura. Rosanna had never in her life stood face to face with an English woman; she had never stepped inside an English woman's home before. Laura was friendly and at least she wore a dress, although the neckline was rather low. Levi disappeared down a hallway and emerged minutes later wearing English clothes. Then he left with Bob to go to the DMV. Laura offered Rosanna tea and they sat in a brightly lit kitchen where Laura began to talk without pause while Rosanna nodded politely, relieved that nothing Laura was saying seemed to require an actual answer.

Laura mentioned her boys, her church, her investment club, bridge club, and bowling league. By the time they had finished two cups of tea, Laura was complaining about the cold Wisconsin winters. "I have seasonal depression but I've bought this amazing lamp for light therapy. Would you like to see how it works?" Laura was just getting up from the table when the pick-up truck roared up the drive out front. The loud rumbling truck heaved to a halt causing Levi's buggy horse to rear up a bit and dance in place.

Rosanna's tentative smile broadened significantly and she stood up and thanked Laura as she put on her coat. Out the window she saw that Levi was already holding the horse's head, calming her down, as Bob bounded up the front steps. He was barely over the threshold when they heard his booming voice. "Levi failed the driving test, a lot of people do. We'll try again next week." Rosanna thanked him nervously as she hurried outside and took the reins from Levi so that he could go inside and change his clothes. Levi was in and out of Bob's house in minutes, dressed in his Amish clothes. All the way home she fought the urge to suggest that he come by himself the next week, but as much as she disliked the idea of spending another afternoon with Laura, she knew it was important that she accompany Levi, and she would.

One week later they took the long trek back to Bob and Laura's, Levi changed clothes, and he and Bob went to the DMV. Laura showed Rosanna into a blue room where two cups and a teapot were set out with a plate of cookies. She was wearing a long skirt the color of raspberries, and a pale blue sweater. Rosanna admired the color combination but she didn't comment, that would show her vanity. They sat on the sofa and Laura began to talk as she poured the tea and offered the cookies.

"There was a time when the logging business failed, back when John was in eighth grade and Peter was in sixth. Bob got a job at a direct mail company in Augusta. It was the night shift and he sorted envelopes, printed labels, whatever his younger boss told him to do, and he hated it. Mostly he didn't like having someone else as his boss. Plus the pay wasn't great, but I found work cleaning houses and we were able to keep up with the mortgage."

Rosanna was suddenly very interested. She set down her cup of tea. "Can you make much money cleaning other people's houses?"

"Oh, sure, everyone around here has outside help. Back then I worked for a cleaning team, a group called The Church Ladies. I knew them from guess where? church of course, and I worked with them for sixteen months until Bob got his logging business back up and running. Three of us would ride around in a pink mini-van that had a big ad painted on the side: Let The Church Ladies make your home shine." She laughed heartily. "Now I have a Mexican girl come here every other week, Salina, and I pay her seventy-five dollars for half a day's work."

Laura moved on to other topics which Rosanna barely heard but she pretended to be engaged, and when

Levi and Bob returned, Rosanna was disappointed for Levi that he had failed the driving test again, but as she thanked Laura for the tea, she couldn't help feeling optimistic, for now she knew what she could do to make money if she left the Amish, clean houses.

In the Spring of 1997, with other Amish co-signing on the loan, Levi and Rosanna borrowed sixty-four thousand dollars from a man in the Amish community to buy an eighty-acre farm about a mile away from Rosanna's parents and six miles from Levi's parents. It was close enough that Rosanna could continue teaching, Levi could still help his father on the family farm as well as continuing to make craft items for The Woodshed, but most importantly, it was close enough that the Amish could keep tabs on them.

Wouldn't they just love the freedom of living on their own and having visitors who weren't Amish? Rosanna began to feel that she might be willing to leave if it was still something Levi intended to do. Although in her heart she dearly hoped and prayed that living separately from his parents would be enough to satisfy him because leaving meant she would be shunned. Could she abide that? She honestly did not know. What she did know was that she liked having her own house with windows that looked out onto her own yard.

And having their own place had made a big difference in their bedroom at night as she had hoped it would. For the first time since she married, Rosanna could reach for Levi in the darkness of their own very private bedroom without worrying that his family might hear them because instead of being right outside her bedroom window, his his family lived six miles away!

One day Levi took the buggy to Augusta and left a note on the door of two young men who had left the Amish, Mose and Aaron. His note said: Come over to my place. I'd like to talk to you. Levi Hochstetler. When they showed up at his house later that week he told them,

"I need driving experience so I can get my license before my permit expires."

They were excited. "You're going to leave again?" Mose said. "Aaron's brother Jacob also left and he's living at a friend's place."

"He just got a car, too," Aaron added.

They agreed to help Levi and after they left, Levi turned to Rosanna. He had a big grin on his face. "This is it," he said.

But less than a week later, the plan fell apart.

Mose, Aaron and Jacob had gone down to a local river known for fast currents and deep fishing holes. They were going to fish from shore, but instead, they got into the water and started swimming. Jacob didn't know how to swim and he accidentally stepped into one of the holes. The others couldn't pull him out, and he drowned. Mose and Aaron were so horrified that they promptly went back to the Amish. They thought Jacob's drowning was a sign because the preachers had warned them that terrible things would happen if they left the Amish.

Levi was sorry about Jacob, and disappointed that Mose and Aaron wouldn't be able to help him learn to drive, but mostly he was afraid that they were going to rat him out, which was exactly what they did. The next Monday morning when his parents pulled into the drive, his father got out of the buggy and said solemnly, "Levi, is it true what we hear, you are leaving?"

"Yes."

Levi heard his mother's whimper rising up from inside the buggy as his father considered him for a moment and then got into the buggy and shook the reins harshly. The horse took off at a fast clip and Levi could hear his mother wail as the buggy pulled out of the drive. He thought about going to school to fetch Rosanna but he was still finishing up his chores when he heard horses approaching and he walked out to the middle of his drive and saw them, two buggies, his parents in front and Rosanna's parents right behind, with a very frightened

Rosanna sandwiched between them on the buggy seat. Her parents had taken her out of school.

All afternoon buggies arrived with elders descending upon Levi and Rosanna beseeching them. "Why can't you do what's right? You're going against what you promised God and the church!" They were unrelenting and Rosanna cried and cried until she couldn't take it anymore. By dusk she had committed to staying Amish, even though Levi remained steadfast in his intention to leave. "But I'm staying with Rosanna," he told everyone.

This meant that Levi was shunned and Rosanna was not.

For two years they lived this way. Rosanna continued to teach school and every other Sunday her parents came by in the horse and buggy to take her to church. Out of respect for Rosanna, Levi dressed Amish at home, but since he was shunned, they couldn't eat at the same table and she couldn't accept anything from his hand. If he wanted to give her a book, or some money, a slip of paper or a piece of pie, he had to set it on the table and she would pick it up. They followed all the rules but one: they shared a bed and had relations more often than before.

Levi continued to make crafts for The Woodshed, too, and within a year, he got his driver's license, he bought a car, and he began working at the direct mail company Bob had worked for once. He liked being employed and getting a paycheck, but he could hardly tolerate the tedious nature of the indoor work. After five months or so, he heard that a construction company was looking for men to help put up pole barns. He showed up and was hired on the spot. He was a strong, skilled laborer, and he enjoyed working outside with the other men. There was a hardy camaraderie he hadn't been able to establish at the direct mail place, and it was an interesting introduction to the way people who weren't Amish kidded each other. One day a co-worker told him, "I own the island of Puerto Rico."

"Really?" Levi asked with amazement. "If you're that rich why are you working here?" He certainly didn't understand. The other man smiled and shrugged and they went back to nailing the trusses in place. About two weeks later Levi pointed that man out to another guy and said, "Did you know he owns an island?"

The other man chortled with amusement. "What, you believed that joker?" He then went about telling everyone in sight, and Levi was chided for being so naïve. He didn't mind though. He laughed along with everyone else. He felt that he was learning so much every single day that his brain was swelling with knowledge. The thought of that made him smile, too. Surely his old hat wouldn't even fit him anymore.

In 1999, one of the guys Levi worked construction with told him that the Federal Prison was hiring. "You get full benefits, health insurance, sick leave, vacation leave, a good salary and paid training." Levi wanted all of those things. He filled out an application and he was hired as a prison guard. Classroom training was two hours away and it lasted for five weeks, then they had on-site training three hours away at the Maximum Security Prison in Waupun.

Levi's six-month probation started in July, and during the week, he stayed with a friend, Noah, who used to be Amish, and his English wife, Joyce. He went home to Rosanna most weekends.

Levi loved the job benefits but the other guards weren't friendly and some were very rough, a little hateful, and often crude. The atmosphere was understandably tense. Once another prison guard spit in Levi's face but he just took it, he didn't want to call any more attention to himself. Deep within he was still Amish, still a pacifist. The inmates on the other hand could be quite cordial. They were masters of manipulation and sensed early on that Levi was unsophisticated. They'd ask about his home life and get him talking about the farm, and soon they'd be requesting that he bring them a box of crackers or a bag of cookies, and he began to worry about what the next request would be.

One day Wayne Shelby, whose nickname was "the librarian," asked Levi to bring him a new paperback. The prison library only had donated books most of them from the last decade.

A book seemed harmless enough. "What book would you like?" Levi asked.

"Anything by Louis L'Amour. Hondo if you can get it, or Showdown at Yellow Butte."

Levi had to write it down and he stumbled over the spelling of the name L'Amour.

"Doesn't that mean love?" somebody called out in a sing-song.

"Ooh, love," others chimed in and there was a lot of kissing noise.

Levi showed his note to Wayne to make sure he'd gotten the name right. "You write like a second-grader!" Wayne said with a smile, and Levi quickly pocketed the note and threw it away when he got back to Noah's. After that he was stand-offish with the inmates, he was all business, and they soon switched their attentions to each other and anyone else who would engage them.

One Saturday when Levi arrived home Rosanna met him in the drive. She threw her arms around him and said through happy tears, "Levi, I'm pregnant!" They were overjoyed and also bemused. All the times they had tried to get pregnant and it took moving off his parents' farm—with him gone all week, too!

When the Amish discovered Rosanna was pregnant some said she should be shunned, but others spoke up. "They are a married couple of course they are going to sleep together." Most in the community didn't want any more of this devilish stuff going on though. The Bishops took a vote in the order and made a pronouncement: "For Rosanna to be a church member in good standing she has to leave Levi." She wanted to do what was right but she did not want to leave him.

One day in her ninth month Levi came home and found that Rosanna's parents had moved her to their house. He drove right over there and her father refused to let him see her. He went back again and again and after a few weeks of this persistence they finally allowed short visits.

"I want to be here for the birth," he told her.

"No, Levi, that's not possible."

"Why?"

"The midwife has refused to come if you are going to be here, because you aren't Amish and she's afraid you'll sue her."

"That's the furthest thing from my mind!" he exclaimed. But instead of arguing, he took the week off when the baby was supposed to be born. He thought the baby would be born at night and so every evening he drove over to his in-laws' house, parked up the road out of sight and went to sleep in the barn knowing that his father-in-law would have to come to the barn to hitch up the horse and buggy to go get the midwife when it was time. Levi would go into the house then and when his father-in-law returned with the midwife, they couldn't make him leave because Rosanna would be in labor. This was his unwavering plan and he slept in the hayloft every night that week. And every night nothing happened, his father-in-law did not hurry to the barn to get the horse and buggy in order to fetch the midwife, so that Levi could run inside and be there to see his baby being born. It did not happen as he had hoped, and the next Monday he had to return to work.

One day the next week Levi's supervisor came for him and said, "You need to go home your wife had a baby."

Rosanna had asked a friend to call Noah, and Noah had called the prison and left a message for Levi. On his way back to Augusta, Levi stopped and bought a camera, even though he didn't know how to use one. He figured that whether his child would be Amish or not, he was going to have a picture of his baby.

When he got to the door, his father-in-law told him, "You can stay one hour." Levi ran up the stairs and Rosanna handed him his baby boy. He was astonished. They had already decided to name a boy Samuel, after Levi's grandfather, the bishop, and as they talked excitedly, admiring their son, the hour went by in a flash.

A week later when Levi returned to visit his son again, Rosanna met him at the door, all teary-eyed. "I can't let you in," she said. "Dad won't let you visit anymore." She looked at him, her eyes pleading. "I don't want this, Levi."

Levi's stance was firm. "Let's just go, Rosanna, grab your things, grab the baby, let's just go."

"I can't."

"Why not?"

"I don't want to hurt Mom that way."

He stood there and said loudly, "I'm going to do what it takes to see my baby."

As he turned to go, he heard his father-in-law's deep voice in the background. "Good news," Rosanna called to him. "Dad says you can see the baby."

Levi strode straight into the house and upstairs to hold Samuel without a passing nod to his in-laws who waited glumly in the kitchen. Once again, he held his baby boy, gazed lovingly at him for almost an hour, and felt completely elated. Upon leaving, Levi walked up to Rosanna's father, faced him straight on, and said, "I want more than this." He didn't wait for a response.

Levi drove three hours back to Waupun and sat down with Noah and Joyce. He told them about the visit and said, "We need to get her out of there." The three of them drove back to Rosanna's house that same day. The men waited in the car and Joyce went up to the door and was allowed inside to visit, as Levi knew she would be. He also knew that Rosanna would walk Joyce to the door when the visit was over and he would be waiting just out of sight around the edge of the doorway.

When the two women appeared, Levi said to Rosanna, "Come with me."

"I can't."

"Just for a week."

She hesitated for a second and then said, "Okay." She got the baby and a few belongings and hurried to the car to climb into the backseat with Joyce.

All the while her father stood in the doorway calling, "Rosanna, don't do this!" Rosanna never went back to the Amish.

Nine

Levi and Rosanna continued to stay with Noah and Joyce while Levi finished his training and six months probation at Waupun Federal Penitentiary and during that time he also volunteered for the prison's Emergency Response Unit which required additional special shot gun training. It was his nature to try new things, to accept difficult challenges and gain wide-ranging experience almost as if he were making up for the lost years when he was Amish.

Rosanna became more and more accustomed to living like the English. Still, they longed to go back to their farm and Levi watched for a transfer closer to home. Finally there was an opening at Black River Falls Medium Security Prison, which was only about forty-five minutes away from Augusta, so they moved home and began to develop an English life there. They attended "The Friends" church every Sunday where Rosanna made some English friends who wore skirts. She had a big garden, she loved being a mother, and she was happy. But Levi was growing weary of working at the prison. In 2001 he quit and began a series of odd jobs. He worked at a furniture factory and a dairy farm, and with his Amish building skills, he was always able to find work in construction.

In 2003, Levi and Rosanna had another baby. Their son Jacob was born in a hospital, and Levi was right there beside Rosanna for the birth. He thought that was completely amazing, especially because it was all paid for by Badger Care state health insurance, a thoroughly English practice that he accepted wholeheartedly. He continued to work at the furniture factory while he began shoeing horses on the side. He got some business cards printed up, advertised himself as a farrier, and before long he had a few regular clients.

Though he saw real potential for working on his own in this manner, what he really wanted was a carriage company. He wanted a fancy carriage led by a team of polished horses and he himself would wear a tuxedo and a top hat. Such an idea was against every Amish notion of living a humble plain life, and perhaps that made him want it more.

In the summer of 2004, Levi attended a spring horse sale in Neillsville, Wisconsin. There were a lot of Amish there. It was a four-day event, Wednesday through Saturday, featuring horse tack, including harnesses and other gear for horse-drawn carriages and wagons, plus all kinds of horses. Levi was interested in a team of percherons called Thunder and Lightning that were listed at three thousand dollars by a young Amish man who was also named Levi, but he didn't bid on them as he didn't have that kind of cash. When the horses were no-saled which meant the seller didn't get his minimum bid, Levi approached the owner afterwards and said, "I'd like to buy your percheron team, give me a month to get the money." The other Levi wasn't supposed to have a cell phone but he had one on the sly and he gave Levi the phone number. "I'll call as soon as I have the money," Levi told him.

True to his word, a month later, Levi had saved up the three thousand and drove two hours to buy Thunder and Lightning, but since he was no longer Amish, the other Levi couldn't accept a check from him. Levi had to write the check to the seller's English buddy and then after the purchase was completed, the other Levi asked to hitch a ride. Levi agreed, but it was exactly that kind of hypocrisy that drove him crazy about the Amish. The guy wasn't allowed to take his check but he could get a ride from him. Levi says, "If they can bend a rule without their father finding out about it, they will."

Shortly after buying Thunder and Lightning, Levi rented a vis-à-vis carriage from a man who had once had the intention of starting a carriage company but never got around to it. It was one of those great plans that never reach fruition. After awhile Levi bought the carriage outright, and he also purchased a six-horse gooseneck trailer that enabled him to haul the horses and the carriage together. His vision was taking hold. They advertised their carriage company and calls began to come in. Rosanna made the appointments for him, and for the next few years, while he was still working at the furniture factory, Levi donned a tuxedo and top hat, hitched Thunder and Lightning to his vis-à-vis carriage and hired out to weddings, parades, Christmas events and birthday parties.

In the latter part of 2004 Levi was working at a construction job, and telling a co-worker about his carriage, horses and big gooseneck trailer, when the guy said, "You know there are people who just haul horses."

"What do you mean, for money?"

"Yeah, there's a website for it and everything."

Levi checked it out. He heard about a man in Michigan whose sole business was hauling horses. Levi contacted him, drove up there, and went on a few jobs with the man. He was excited about the possibility of hauling horses for a living, and it wasn't too long before he went out on his own.

The way it worked was people would post on a website called Traveling Horse.com. They'd say where the horse was to be picked up and where he was to be delivered, and horse-haulers would bid on the job. At first Levi couldn't get any jobs, but finally he got a gig taking a horse from Wisconsin to the Second Wind Horse adoption agency in West Virginia. Second Wind started throwing a lot of business his way. He picked up a dressage horse in Maryland, took the horse to Second Wind for a month then delivered the same horse to its new home in California. Levi says, "I would send two to three hundred emails a day bidding on jobs. I had to pay a member fee to use the website, and the standard hauling fee could range between fifty cents to ninety cents per mile. A loaded mile is one way, and a running mile is round trip."

He loved the freedom of being on the open road, of being his own boss, and the work became plentiful. As for Rosanna, she had liked doing scheduling for the carriage business and would go on some carriage jobs with him, but when he started hauling horses she was out of the picture completely and he would be gone for weeks at a time. He'd come home and the first thing she'd ask was, "When are you leaving again?" About the only thing they would talk about to each other was their boys and they started arguing about discipline. Their marriage, which had always been somewhat fragile, began to fall apart.

On the road he encountered some dangerous mishaps, as well. Late one spring evening the trailer blew a tire. There he was lying on his side under the trailer, on the left-hand shoulder of the Los Angeles Freeway. It was difficult and perilous as traffic peeled by in a continuous whir and he was astonished that not a single person stopped to ask if he needed help.

Worse was the time he was hauling horses along the coast of California in the dark when the trailer dropped over the side of a cliff. Two tires on the right side were sheared off and it cost him eight hundred dollars to get the truck and trailer off the cliff and three weeks for repairs. He camped out on the Pacific beach the entire time while he waited to get his truck and trailer back.

But the most terrible thing that happened to him was during a Wisconsin to Florida run. Levi had gotten to know a horse broker in California who told him about a horse transporter in Iowa who wanted a driving partner for a trip from Wisconsin to Florida and back. They'd be hauling horses, donkeys and sheep and they'd use the other man's rig. Levi would help with driving for a fee.

Late one night Levi was at the wheel driving on Interstate 75 through the southern part of Kentucky towards Knoxville, Tennessee. The rig's owner was asleep in the backseat. It was the dead of night when Levi saw a car coming up behind them. It was moving erratically and nearly sideswiped their trailer. The driver of the erratic car overcorrected, swerved and fishtailed, spun out of control, and bashed into the left front corner of the truck Levi was driving before coming to a sudden stop in the median. The impact sent the rig Levi was driving into the guard rail where the truck mowed off a good four to five hundred feet before careening down the embankment with the trailer pushing the truck sideways. They came to a stop about seventy feet downhill from the highway in a ravine.

Levi wasn't hurt too bad but the rig's owner broke a bone in his foot. Miraculously though, none of the animals were injured. The fire department called a guy with a livestock trailer to come reload the animals and take them to his place about ten miles away. Transport would then be arranged to take the animals the rest of the way to Florida.

The rig's owner videotaped his totaled truck and trailer, the embankment, the mangled guard rail, and even tire tracks on the highway and then they transferred all of their stuff into the trunks of two police cars before a wrecker pulled everything out and went on its way. The police took Levi and the rig's owner to a car rental place in Knoxville and since Levi was the only one who had a credit card, he rented a car. They moved all their stuff, most of it belonging to the owner of the wrecked rig from the police cars to the rental car and it was packed to the ceiling. When they started the long drive back to Iowa, Levi was at the wheel, and the other guy dozed beside him. It was still pitch black outside when Levi drove a little too far to the right a few times, he ran over the white line that marked the shoulder, but he never hit the ridge marks. All of a sudden, the other guy completely flipped out. He grabbed Levi and screamed in his face. "Pull over you incestuous Amish piece of shit. Stop the car. I'm driving."

Levi flipped on the blinkers, yanked the wheel, stomped on the brake, and lurched to a stop on the shoulder. He threw open his door, got out and walked around the car. As he switched places with the other guy, he was inwardly shaking, but he refused to meet the man's eyes. He got into the passenger seat and the other guy swung back out onto the road.

Levi didn't say a word. He pretended to sleep all the while seething inside and thinking, no one talks to me that way. When the other guy pulled into a rest stop and got out to go to the bathroom, he left the keys in the ignition as Levi had hoped he would. Levi slid over and took off. He stopped at the next police station he came to and told them what happened. "I'm afraid he's going to kill me," he said. "I don't want to see him again."

The police radioed to a patrol car in the vicinity to meet the guy Levi had left behind at the rest stop. Levi drove back there and unloaded all of the guy's stuff into the patrol car without saying one word to the man or even looking at him. He drove the rest of the way home by himself.

When he got back to Wisconsin, he told Rosanna some of what happened but not exactly what the man had said to him. He was home about a week before he went out on another job and he kept as busy as he could. Not only did they need the money, but he liked working. His schedule was fairly constant; he'd be gone two to three weeks and home for a week and a half. Rosanna liked the money he was bringing in but that was about all. They continued to argue over disciplining their sons. He thought she was too easy on them and he told her, "Let's just don't disagree in front of them." But she would argue with him in front of the boys time and again, and almost every argument would end with her asking him, "When are you going again?"

Rosanna and Levi separated in 2006. When the Amish found out, they came in and tried to take her back but she wouldn't go. She was upset when Levi said he wanted a divorce, and she asked him to wait a few months. "Don't tell anyone, please Levi," she asked.

Rosanna filed for divorce three weeks later. Her friends had told her she had to file for divorce so he wouldn't take the children from her.

Levi said with astonishment, "Shoot Rosanna, I'm not going to take the kids from you. You're the primary caregiver, you have the ability to take care of them; I'm on the road or working all the time. I would never take them from you." He was furious that her friends at church were advising her like that. He thought they had overstepped and he was just floored at the way it all happened.

For six months Levi continued transporting horses but then he had to stop. The child support payment was too much, especially on top of his mortgage, insurance, and loans on his trucks. He took on some odd jobs and then moved to Anderson, South Carolina where he went to work for The Barnum and Bailey Circus. "It was a union job and I was on the floor crew. During shows we'd set up one act in total darkness (we wore all black) while another act was under the spotlight. We had no time off and lived on the train. Each of us had our own little five-by-eight-foot cell where we kept our stuff. The other crew members argued and yelled and cussed at each other constantly. I couldn't take it and quit after nine days."

He looked for work on the Internet. His first priority was to find a job that would enable him to keep up with his child support, alimony and other financial responsibilities. Two jobs he applied for couldn't have been more different: Ranch manager in South Dakota and Assistant Barn manager in Upperville, Virginia. He decided to accept whichever offer came in first and that's how he ended up moving to Virginia.

"I couldn't believe my eyes when I got to Upperville," Levi says. "There were miles and miles of black board fencing and stone walls, green rolling hills and the Blue Ridge Mountains always in view. It was breathtaking. The place where I was working had recently been purchased, eleven-hundred acres for twenty-two million. The movie "Gone with the Wind" was filmed there."

It was a large polo pony estate. His job was to feed and turn out the horses, muck the stalls, and care for foals and yearlings. He lasted three months. He and the Irish female manager had clashing personalities.

About twenty miles away in Bluemont, Virginia, he found work at a farrier business called Forging Ahead. He was an apprentice there for two years full time, then he got his own clients and worked part time for Forging Ahead before going out on his own. Throughout it all he continued to support his sons and met his other financial obligations, and he sees his sons Samuel and Jacob whenever he is able. Rosanna is the primary parent in Wisconsin, and she works cleaning houses for others.

In 2007, Levi and Rosanna sold their farm and Levi recalls with a little bitterness that when he went to pay off the loan, the Amish lender wouldn't look at him or speak to him. The man glared and pointed to the table. Levi placed the check there and left, knowing there was no point in even saying goodbye.

In the fall of 2009, Levi purchased The Shenandoah Carriage Company. He still has Thunder and Lightning and his vis-à-vis carriage, as well as Doc and Dan, a pair of haflingers [draft ponies], and another carriage that came with the business. He recently bought another team of draft horses, too, bringing his total to six. He continues the farrier work, and hopes to own the carriage business outright in a few years.

In 2012 he became engaged to a woman he met in Purcellville. He had seen her jogging in town and he just happened to have some flyers advertising a charity race. He sought her out to give her the flyer, they started talking, and they've been together ever since. They hope to buy their own farm in Virginia one day.

Throughout all the changes in Levi's life and the many moves from place to place and state to state, he has carried with him the wagon his grandfather made for him when he was five, which he hopes to turn into a coffee table. He also has his Amish clothes and even his prison guard uniform!

Levi's memory for dates and events is impeccable and his desire to have his story known, even made into a movie, is far-reaching. When I joked that maybe Steven Spielberg could make the movie, Levi said in all seriousness, "If Steven Spielberg made a movie of my life that would be a dream-come-true!"

Afterward
The Amish Way of Life as Seen from the Outside

A Note from the Author

Both of my daughters sang in the Virginia Women's Chorus at the University of Virginia, and every concert concluded with the Shaker hymn, "Simple Gifts."

> 'Tis a gift to be simple, 'tis a gift to be free
> 'Tis a gift to come down to where we ought to be,
> And when we find ourselves in the place just right,
> 'Twill be in the valley of love and delight.

    Sweet enchanting voices would start out like a hum, swelling and soon soaring, filling the gorgeous rafters of the chapel with otherworldly song, reaching out and drawing us in, then receding, soothing, calming us down only to fill us again as heavenly harmonies started over in a different octave, four times or five, bringing tears to our eyes, tears of remembrance for pasts we hadn't known, and places we may have seen only in dreams.
    This sense of calm and the longing for another time is what happens to many people when they travel to Amish country and see a black boxy buggy up ahead, the elegant harnessed horse bravely and earnestly trotting along asphalt roads breathing in gas fumes and dust from passing trucks, buses and cars, sometimes honked at, often leered at. The faces inside the buggy are serene and peaceful, we imagine, but they are shielded by wide brimmed hats or delicate bonnets, eyes forward, seemingly unaware of the gawkers, looking almost like figures in a wax museum, as if their quaint presence

alongside our modern whirl is part of the scenery, and they are out there just for our viewing and analysis.

"Look at the Amish, so picturesque in their old-fashioned costumes, honest and hard-working, amazing aren't they?" Most of us don't wish to be like them but we admire what we think they represent and we're in awe of their fortitude, the perseverance and effort it must take to resist change. They don't flaunt their religion; they seem to live it so flawlessly that unless you think about it you may not be aware that being true to their faith informs their every breath and step.

Tourists may assume that all Amish are alike in their beliefs and practices, but that is far from the truth. Neighboring Amish settlements can be nearly as different from each other as the Amish are from the English, which is how they refer to anyone or anything not Amish.

The Amish had split from the Mennonites, and before that, both Anabaptist groups had split from the Roman Catholics in order to worship in the right way as they deemed it to be. Amish individuals are baptized at about seventeen years of age, when they are considered adult and able to commit to the church. A few sects have Rumspringa, when youth are able to experiment with outside influences—Levi's settlement did not. Venturing out was not offered by Levi's very strict Old Order Amish sect and any sort of experimentation or "acting English" was condemned. Amish settlements continually split and divide even now, and each group has its particular tenets.

> All sects are different, because they come from men; morality is everywhere the same, because it comes from God. [Voltaire]

Levi says the Amish don't act true to their hearts, they base their actions on what the church wills and this was a difference he felt from an early age when he thought to himself, Why am I Amish? I shouldn't be Amish.

"They behave according to what they think they need to do to get to heaven," he explains. For example, Levi goes back to see his parents every year with his boys and on several occasions they have been allowed into the house for a visit, but other times they have been refused.

"Why?" I want to know.

"They're afraid of getting in trouble with the church," he says. "If they let me come back and eat with them or spend the night they'd have to confess at the members meeting because I was once a church member but am no more. The rule is not to have anything to do with those people—people like me.

"One year I pulled up to the barn and the boys and I went up to the house and knocked on the door. No one answered. We were heading back to the car when my dad came out of the machine shed.

"My dad asked me, Wie bist du? That's how are you? He speaks to me in German but switches to English for the boys."

[Amish German is also known as Pennsylvania Dutch. In Levi's community the Amish speak German at home and English at school, except on Fridays, when they speak German even on the playground and read the German Bible.]

"Some who have left the Amish refuse to speak German because they think it means the Amish still have a hold over them," Levi says as an aside. "But I want to maintain my heritage."

"So," he continues. "I asked my Dad, is Mom home? He said, Yes, she's in the store. My parents started an Amish store after I left. I asked, can we see her? He said, No, I think as long as you choose to keep on living this way I don't want you to see her. We don't want you to come around."

In his book Amish Society, John Hostetler explains that for the Amish, salvation is found in a community of those who withdraw from affairs of mankind.

"Do you hug your parents, Levi?" I asked him.

"I hug my mother, but she doesn't hug me back. I just want to wrap my arms around her." Levi shakes his head sadly, and then he shrugs, his expression accepting. We look at each other across the kitchen table. I know it doesn't matter how old a person is, Levi's in his late thirties, and I'm in my late fifties. Where our parents are concerned, we will always know how it felt to be a little child.

"Mommy!" I cry, throwing my arms out wide and we share a laugh.

I'm sentimental in that regard because my parents died so many years ago, my mother when I was sixteen and my father when I was thirty-two. A few years after my mother died my father married a woman who had her own big family and my siblings and I weren't exactly ostracized, but we didn't see him much after that, or each other. So I have some understanding of how it feels to be cut off from your family and past.

Levi's most precious possessions include two quilts his mother made for him, a wagon his grandfather made for him, and a slide rocker his parents made for each of the children, but since Levi had left the Amish by then, his parents gave his rocker to his wife because at the time she was still Amish. When Levi and Rosanna divorced he took the rocker, which made her mad—but it was mine, he tells me as if he needs to justify it. He also treasures a black and white photo a friend took of his parents when they weren't looking. The Amish don't like to be photographed.

Levi criticizes the Amish for being hypocritical. "Some will blatantly break the rules and it's okay as long as the church doesn't find out, but members are expected to confess their sins before the congregation, even those things you do by yourself that nobody knows about." He looks down at his lap before stumbling over the words. "I'm not sure how to say it, ejaculation," he finally admits.

Although masturbation is practically heralded in popular culture, boasted about on TV sit-coms, lauded in the musical Hair, laughingly recounted tongue-in-cheek by Frank McCourt in his prize-winning memoir Angela's Ashes, I doubt there are many who would, if given the choice, choose to stand before their parents, neighbors and friends and admit to such acts—especially since such an act is against church rules and therefore serves as an obstacle to heaven, not just for the individual, but for the entire community.

Yet it wasn't simply the torment of having to make such a confession that drove Levi away from the Amish, it was having to listen to other people confess week after week. Even Catholic priests hearing confessions one-on-one in a private booth veiled in darkness find such a task nerve-racking and priests have seminary training, workshops and retreats to develop coping strategies.

Levi describes the ritual as if he'd just experienced it last Sunday, and not fifteen years ago. "The church service is three hours long, followed by lunch, then the members' meeting. Before the meeting you tell the deacon what your confession is, he confers with the ministers and bishop, and comes back to tell you the level of your confession. Level 1 is saying it out loud while sitting on the first bench in front of the members. Level 2 is kneeling before the congregation and confessing. I can't remember what Level 3 is, but Level 4 is shunning. Premarital sex is a shunning offense."

For twenty-one years Levi had lived by the rigid rules of his Amish community—he had been a good Amish man, and when it was discovered that he had left on purpose, the community was surprised, they were unaware of his unhappiness because he had never acted out. In fact one of his aunts said, "I thought if anyone were to leave it would be Samuel (Levi's older brother)."

Until the moment Levi ran off into the night—an escape he'd orchestrated to look like a bloody abduction, stealing English clothes ahead of time, locating a getaway car, telling no one, not even his wife, for fear they'd confess, Levi had faithfully followed the doctrine of his church and community, yet he felt increasingly constricted and limited in his options. As he put it, "I was married, but doing what I'd always done, and living right next door to my parents."

Levi is an independent thinker, quite intelligent, and four years of attending the members meeting and listening to the embarrassing and annoying confessions had gotten to be too much. Setting up his escape to look like an abduction was an attempt to somehow leave his family out of it, so his desertion wouldn't reflect poorly on them, and it was also an act of rebellion against the mandatory confessionals, if he didn't leave of his own volition, then he wouldn't have to confess to it. His plan didn't make a lot of sense but given his limited knowledge of the ways of the outside world, and the fact that he was so young, I can see the logic in it. The dramatic scene he created is exactly what I might cook up if I were a teenage boy. One thing about his plan that went wrong, that his getaway car turned out to be a junker, was a relief to Levi in retrospect. "If I'd stolen a car," he said recently, "I'd be in jail."

...

Another prevalent reason men and women leave the Amish is to pursue higher education, because the Amish only go through the eighth grade. And then there are those who leave because of religious differences, just as their ancestors did.

"We stepped out because we wanted to follow God's rules," says a woman in her forties, referring to herself, her husband and their seven children. Her family had left an Old Order Amish settlement five months before in the fall of 2011. [She doesn't want her name used.]

"Can you tell me what you mean by that?" I asked.

"Amish don't open up to God's word as the Bible says."

Not being religious myself (I was raised Presbyterian but that was a very long time ago), I didn't exactly understand, but having spoken to Levi at length about his Amish upbringing, I had an idea she was referring to the Amish belief that living Amish is the right way to live and the way others live is wrong. Moreover, to have anything to do with others, especially someone like Levi who had once been an Amish church member would threaten their own salvation. As Levi says, "You don't look at those people."

I moved on, knowing I was not prepared to discuss theology with the formerly Amish woman. "What was good about growing up Amish?" I asked her.

"We learned to work hard at what we need to do to make a living, for me it was cooking, baking and sewing. I love to sew."

"I do, too," I said. "One more thing, Levi talks about the fear of man, that his parents have the fear of man, do you know what he means by that?"

"That's being afraid of what somebody else is saying about you, not what God says, being afraid of getting in trouble with the church."

"How does it feel to be shunned?" I asked her.

"We're all right because we have God."

And that's all she had to say about that, but I knew, because Levi had told me, that she had gone to visit her parents once after leaving the Amish and her father had told her, "I don't want you to bring the children around anymore, and don't you visit us either."

Levi once asked his father, a minister, "If this church is really God's church, and living this way will get us to heaven, then why is there so much turmoil at church?"

His father said, "I really don't know, I wish things were different."

What really sets Levi's story apart from other books about leaving the Amish is that he lived Amish and suffered the consequences of leaving the Amish but he still cherishes many aspects of his Amish upbringing. "I want my sons to know all my life experiences," he says, "how it was for me. But I never wished my sons were brought up Amish, I don't want them to feel that it is so wrong to live life how others live. I want them to be well-adjusted and accustomed to today's lifestyle yet, I want them to have good morals. I think having daily chores and responsibilities as a kid is very important."

"How do you think your sons would feel if you suddenly took them back to live like the Amish?" I asked.

"They'd complain about all the stuff they can't have," he said with a grin. "Being raised Amish prepared me for life but sometimes I feel cheated because I don't have my parents to fall back on emotionally or financially. Still, I have the best of both worlds. I love the lifestyle I live, but the foundation my parents instilled guides me, structures my thinking and drives me on a daily basis."

How I Met Levi

People often ask how I met Levi. In December of 2009, my husband, Mark, had run an ad on Craigslist offering round bales of orchard grass hay for sale. Levi's was the fourth "hay" message of the day.

The first message was from a man named Bobby Levison. He sounded local; his words were flat and drawn out, polite but businesslike, and he said he'd call back. The second and third messages were left by women, hard-speaking and brusque—what I've come to deem "horsewomen." Each began her message with a demand to know what kind of hay it was and whether it was suitable for horses, even though the ad clearly said horse quality orchard grass. And each left just a first name and a command to "Call me on my cell," followed by a quick spate of numbers.

Then there was Levi's—full name spoken clearly in an announcer's voice, phone number recited very slowly. His enunciation was careful, his attitude more formal than businesslike, and his manner of speaking was unlike any we normally heard in the Virginia countryside where we live.

I wrote down the messages and left them on the kitchen table for Mark. Depending upon when he got home, he might return the calls that evening. He has a two-hour commute, if the trains are running on time, to a desk job on Capitol Hill. Often the commute is longer if the weather is too hot, too cold, too windy or rainy, or if a freight train is in the way. Freight takes precedence over commuters, since the track is owned by CSX, so it isn't the least bit unusual for the commuter train to rattle along at a snail's pace behind a freight train, or to just plain stop and sit idle because a freight train is expected or broken down. Sometimes obstacles on the track hold up the train; a tree, a power line, or, sadly, a human body. More suicides by train have occurred in recent years, and it feels horribly harsh to consider another person's death an inconvenience, but this is what it boils down to when the journey home is delayed after a very long day.

More than once I've gotten an email from Mark that says: Trains aren't running. Body on the tracks. We're going to figure something out. This means that he and his train buddies will take the subway as far as they can, then hail a cab. The cab fare to the Brunswick station where they park their cars tops a hundred dollars, and none of them are rolling in money, but it's better than waiting at the Rockville Station for promised busses that sometimes don't show up for hours.

Mark only has to worry about his own poor self; many of the other passengers have children to pick up at daycare or school and the late fee rises by the minute. They often miss their children's sporting events or other extracurricular activities, because the train is so unreliable. Still, Mark's desire to get home is just as strong as anyone's.

By five o'clock sleet clicked against the windowpane. It was cold for December and the ten inches of snowfall from the week before formed a slick frosting on the ground that hardened into ice every night as the temperature dropped. We live on a dirt road and we have a gravel-dirt drive, so driving conditions right around our farm aren't bad. But Mark parks at a train station almost seventeen miles away, and black ice is a particular hazard on paved roads. Even longtime farmers and truckers get stuck in the snow or slide off the road.

By 5:45, Mark had just sat down with the mail and a beer when the phone rang. The wall phone is right next to his place at the kitchen table. He picked it up on the second ring. I was washing lettuce at the sink and listening to his side of the conversation. I could tell he was talking to someone about hay. He gave directions to our place and said, "I'll see you around nine."

"That was Levi," he said when he hung up. "He wants to stop by in the morning and get a few bales. Then he's coming back in the afternoon for more."

I glanced over my shoulder and watched him flip through the mail and leave it in a loose stack. Must be junk, I thought. Bills were opened immediately and a comment was always made, then he'd write the due date on the envelope and file it in the knife tray.

"Levi Hochstetler," he pronounced stiffly. "What kind of name do you think that is?"

"Probably German." I turned around to face him, leaning my back against the sink. We carried on many conversations in this manner, with me pausing during dinner preparations, and Mark sipping a beer or a glass of wine (or on really hard days a bourbon) at the kitchen table.

"I guess." Mark scanned the front page of the local paper and tossed it aside. "He just moved into a place on Ashby Farm Circle."

"Really!" That was interesting because Ashby Farm was the next street down from ours. While the Craigslist ad shows our location as Purcellville, people call from all over Loudoun County, and one fellow even came across the river on the ferry from Maryland to buy hay. Our best client though is our next-door neighbor, Robert, who drives his tractor across the hayfield to pick up round bales, one by one, with his German shepherd, Otto, running alongside. Now it seemed likely we'd have another neighbor for a customer.

"How many does he want?"

"Ten to twelve. He has draft horses and they go through a round bale a day."

"Good grief!" Our round bales are about 4X5 feet and one bale serves our five horses a good deal longer than a single day. At our place, the round bale sits out like a continuous buffet during winter. In addition, we give our horses two meals a day: a bucket of grain each, and a square bale to share. We are hay-rich, since we grow our own.

I got a salmon fillet out of the fridge, rinsed it, drizzled lemon juice over it, then chopped ginger and garlic to sprinkle on top, along with a liberal dose of cayenne pepper and turmeric. I put the fish in a roaster with some quartered red potatoes tossed in olive oil, sprinkled salt and pepper over everything, and popped it in the oven.

It was almost six o'clock and Mark was typically starved at dinner time, since he only ate yogurt for lunch. I'm a free-lancer, I work mostly from home, and our children are grown, so I only have Mark to consider. I try to have his dinner ready by 6:30—this is what he has requested time and again—though we usually eat closer to seven.

I washed and cut up a bell pepper, tossed it with red leaf lettuce, threw in a handful of cherry tomatoes, and added dressing, all the while trying to picture which house across the way might belong to Levi. The next time I ventured out to the store, I'd do a quick drive-by on Ashby Farm Circle. Draft horses would be easy to spot and I was just that nosy.

...

Ashby Farm is an enclave of ten year-old custom-built houses on lots ranging from three to twenty-five acres. By contrast, we have thirty-five acres, and our 1890s farm house is surrounded by older barns. The stone-based bank barn is from about 1930, built from trees milled right on the property. The ramshackle corn crib is circa 1910, and its renovation is a never-ending project. The horse barn has hand-cut beams and is our oldest structure, dating from about 1850 to 1875. When we moved here in 1998 this barn was five feet deep in solidified cow manure and the loft was jammed with hay that hadn't seen the light of day for twenty years. The farm had been abandoned and the house hadn't been inhabited for at least five years. The entire property was hidden from view by a stand of thirty-foot tall bamboo.

Every weekend for a year Mark drove out by himself and worked on the house. We had taken a second mortgage on our Arlington home, where we had raised our children, and once the farm was ready we planned to sell the house in Arlington and make the move. The farm has a long view of the Blue Ridge Mountains, Harpers Ferry Gap, and Short Hill Mountain. The house is situated near the center of the property, so it has fields and trees on all sides. After we moved, Mark continued to cut away the bamboo until it was mostly gone, but like poison ivy, it returns en masse each spring. I call him Don Quixote when he goes out with his machete to hack at new bamboo shoots.

We think our place is beautiful. We love the fact that all of the buildings are old, and because of the layout of the land and buildings, no one can ever be any closer to us than they are now. A conservation easement prohibits the land from being subdivided, and our land use designation gives us a nice tax break. Mark still works in D.C. four days a week and eleven years of commuting four hours a day has taken its toll on him, but he loves living here. He dreams of retirement so he can be a full-time farmer.

The next morning, Saturday, I saw Mark's pick-up heading down the drive at about 8 a.m. This is our arrangement. Weekday mornings, he's out the door at 5 a.m. to catch the train; on weekends, he likes to read the paper and drink coffee by himself. And I certainly don't mind languishing in bed until I hear the gate latch click indicating his departure. Saturday mornings he goes to the high school parking lot where the Ruritans charge two dollars a bag for our trash. It's less expensive than paying for trash pick-up and the money goes to a good cause. After that he has no end of errands—Southern States, John Deere, Nichol's Hardware, the gas station. I often don't see him until lunch time unless he's bought some novelty at a yard sale that he wants to show me. Sunday mornings he has an array of chores, too, either household or farm. Except on Sundays he makes breakfast for the dogs and me before he disappears: pancakes, French toast, or waffles.

When he returned from town and came inside to warm up with some toast and apple butter, I asked him what Levi was like. "I don't know," he said between bites. "He's younger than we are. Oh, and he's a farrier. He's going to do trims on the horses next week in exchange for six more rolls." We both smiled. Bartering always pleased us. "That's why he only took a few bales this morning. He has a job at a barn in Charlestown. He'll be back around four to pick up another load. He'll probably have to make two trips this afternoon."

That afternoon, the dogs' riotous barking announced Levi's arrival. Mark went out to meet him at the end of the house drive. From there they'd ride together to the bank barn, and Mark would get on the tractor and lead the way across the hayfield to the fence line where fifty-some bales were lined up side by side.

I was in the kitchen putting together a pan of lasagna for dinner. I glanced out the window from time to time. Normally, it was fifteen minutes to a half an hour before I'd see a truck and laden-down trailer roll back down the driveway and make the difficult turn onto the road. Soon after, Mark would put the tractor away and come inside.

After thirty-five years of marriage, I knew all too well that hunger could grab hold of my husband quite suddenly, rendering him irrational. I wondered how long it would take for Levi to make two trips, and thought about running outside with a snack for Mark after I saw Levi leave with the first load.

I finished assembling the lasagna, covered it and put it in the fridge. Then I went out to feed the horses and barn cats. I was out at the horse barn when Levi came through for the second load. Somehow I had missed the first transaction. He waved and I waved back. It was far too cold to linger, so after I mucked out the barn and refilled the water trough, I hurried back inside. It was nearly five by then and darkness was beginning to fall. After I fed the dogs, I pulled out the cookbook and found a recipe for Italian bread. I especially enjoy baking in the winter time, filling the house with warmth and the heavenly smell of yeast.

I mixed and kneaded the dough and put it aside to rise. It was now officially dark out the window. I poured myself a glass of wine, and flipped through the latest National Geographic looking at the pictures. When I had glanced at every page and studied a few, I went back to the first article and tried to read about the mysteries of the Maya, but it was hard to concentrate.

At 5:30 I pre-heated the oven. Lasagna only took forty-five minutes but it was always better if it sat out afterwards to rest. I punched down the bread dough so it would rise a second time and decided to make garlic butter. Mark would probably be famished when he came inside, but he'd also be pleased. He took enormous satisfaction from growing and selling hay.

A half-hour later, I made a salad. By 6:20 dinner was ready but the dogs were on their beds rather than barking at the door to be let outside, as they'd be if a truck and hay-laden trailer was exiting down the drive. Also, there was still no hungry self-satisfied husband at the door. I looked out the dining room window which had a view of the hay bales, but all I could see were headlights and taillights. I watched for awhile but saw no movement. The vehicles were idling in the snow. I also couldn't see any men's silhouettes. I was curious, but not enough to venture out. I suspected Mark was having tractor trouble.

When the dogs did begin barking to beat the band, I let them outside, and then went to peer out the kitchen window. Canine hearing is uncanny. After awhile headlights loomed beyond the corncrib and I watched the snail-like progress of a pick-up truck pulling a trailer. It appeared to be loaded with round bales, two-deep. The procession cast elongated camel hump shadows on the snow bank as the dark vehicles bobbed over the rutted frozen snow. Mark came in about ten minutes later.

"What on earth took so long?" I asked.

He untied his gumboots and toed them off as he shed his coat. "After he left with the first load I turned the tractor off. Then when he came back, I couldn't get it started. It's just too cold. I may have to get a new battery. I can't believe he didn't give up and leave; it must be about fifteen degrees out there." Mark propped his icy stiff coat against the door frame.

"If the tractor died, then how did he get all that hay loaded?"

"Robert was out checking on his stock, and he came over on his tractor to see what was going on. He loaded Levi's trailer." We both remarked on Levi's perseverance; as well as Robert's good will.

I took the bread out of the oven and set it on the cutting board, then got plates down from the cupboard. I lifted the tin foil off the lasagna pan. "So what's Levi like?"

Mark unfolded the cuffs of his jeans and shook out the hay. Then he washed his hands and made himself a drink. "He's nice." He set the glass on the table, and sat down tiredly. "He drove like a kid who was just learning to drive. He went about three miles an hour." He shook his head in disbelief.

"Maybe it's a new truck," I suggested, smiling, though I had seen plenty of new fancy SUVs hauling new trailers bumpity-bump across the field, splashing through puddles, taking turns a bit fast on the slippery grass or snow. People in farm trucks with jerry-rigged trailers were even more careless.

"No, it's a '95. He's just really, really careful. What're we having?"

He could plainly see what we were having but I answered him anyway. "Lasagna and homemade bread."

The next Saturday, Mark and I were in the paddock by the barn when Levi pulled up in a dark blue Ford F250. We had gone out ten minutes earlier to halter the horses. Farriers and vets are typically late because unless you're first on the list they can be held up for all sorts of reasons at the previous job. Still, you have to be ready for them. Levi was right on time. He got out and said a hearty hello as he went to the back of his truck and opened the metal cabinet doors that stood in place of a tailgate. I noticed that he wasn't very tall, but he was solidly built. He wore a dark blue knit cap over short black hair, a brown canvas barn coat, jeans and heavy boots. He was clean-shaven, with a straight, sunburned nose, interested blue eyes, and a friendly grin.

After I introduced myself, I said, "We thought we'd start with these three." I gestured to the horses behind us. Mark had Danny and Justy both on lead ropes. They are our original horses. Danny is twenty. He's a big red quarter horse with a white blaze. Justy is sixteen. He's dark brown with black legs and a very thick black mane and tail, and he has a white snip on his long nose. He's an appendix, which is half thoroughbred and half quarterhorse. His mama was a barrel racer and he has a lot of spunk, with a quarter horse's playfulness and a thoroughbred's kindness. We've had Danny and Justy for over ten years and they're good boys. Justy would put up a bit of resistance because he was a teenager, but they are both very manageable.

Little Annie is a different story. She's a small sorrel pony mare, built like a tank after a year with us; and she will forever have what I like to refer to as the Scarlett O'Hara syndrome: "With God as my witness, I shall never go hungry again." She eats all the time, a characteristic common, our vet says, of horses who had once been starved.

Annie was rescued from a trailer park junkyard and she has the scars and distrust to prove it. We adopted her after fostering her for six months and she has calmed down immensely but she's still very flighty. She typically shies away from strangers, especially men, and she has an extreme aversion to horse trailers. Just the sound of Levi's truck coming up the drive sent her into a high gallop across the top of the yard. Though she has a halter on, I am already worried about catching her as she enjoys the game of chase and likes nothing better than to run away from me kicking up her heels.

I wished I had put her in a stall, but all we have are webbed stall guards that she pushes against with her stocky chest until the hooks break off. I watched her slip-sliding about showing off her freedom and knew I had only myself to blame for the trouble ahead.

It was every bit as cold that day as it had been the night Levi came to pick up hay, and we'd had another snowfall since then, which brought the accumulation to about 15 inches. My fingers were already starting to burn with pain. I tucked my gloved hands under Danny's mane for warmth, and watched Levi come in through the paddock gate carrying his gear—a large wooden tool box and a metal hoof stand, and he had put on a suede farrier's apron. Our horses didn't wear shoes, which is called 'going barefoot,' but they still needed to have their hooves trimmed and filed; and the frog, a soft v-shaped structure on the underside of each hoof, often needed to be cut back as well. Hoof trims aren't something we can do ourselves even if we had strong backs, for it is surely back-breaking work. It is also highly skilled; a good farrier can call your attention to a horse's potential health problems and injuries.

Levi set his gear down next to Danny and rubbed his neck as he said, "Hey fella, what's your name?"

"This is Danny," I said. "He's the boss."

Levi turned his smiling eyes on me. "I have a Dan, too."

He wasn't wearing gloves, and he didn't seem to mind the cold in the least. He didn't shrug his shoulders in a mock shiver, rub his hands together briskly or stomp his feet to get the feeling back in them, as I was doing. He leaned over, ran his hand down Danny's left front leg, gently squeezed above the fetlock and when Danny lifted his hoof, Levi gripped it confidently and began to clean it out with the hoof pick. Afterwards, he took a long brush that reminded me of a shoe brush and briskly swiped debris off the bottom of the hoof. Then he clamped Danny's leg between his own knees, took up big clippers, and cut all the way around the hoof. He readjusted his hold, switched the clippers for the metal rasp, and filed the edges smooth. The final inspection involved pulling Danny's front leg out and placing the hoof on the metal stand for a finishing. It's important for the hooves to be even, in order for the horse to be balanced.

    I've never been able to stand quietly while a farrier worked. It seems rude to me not to make conversation. Most farriers, like dentists, are very talkative, but Levi was intent on his work. He looked to be in his twenties, and as I watched him work, I couldn't help wondering how he could afford the brick manor home with pond and gazebo, center aisle barn and riding ring. It was the only place on Ashby Farm Circle where I'd seen draft horses grazing—two black percherons on one side of the asphalt drive and two golden haflingers on the other. I had gone slightly out of my way earlier in the week out of blatant curiosity—as I knew I would.

    "How many horses do you have?" I asked.

    "Four at the moment, but I'm looking for another pair." He went from hoof to hoof, effortlessly switching out tools. Danny co-operated and his four feet were trimmed in no time. At one point Annie trotted over stopped short about five feet away and snorted. Levi put down Danny's back hoof and walked up to her, holding out his hand and speaking softly. She stood perfectly still until he touched her nose, then she bolted, slipped in the snow, fell on her side, jumped up and galloped away, holding her tail in a high plume. We laughed. Levi's smile made him look about ten years younger.

    We watched Annie's antics for a bit, enjoying the sheer silliness of it, as well as her beauty. "She's only had her feet done twice before," I said. "She's a rescue. I'm a little apprehensive." I was very apprehensive, but that is my nature.

"Oh, she'll be all right," Mark intervened.

While Mark held Justy's lead rope, Levi filed and trimmed each of Justy's hooves, managing nicely. Justy playfully set his back foot down a few times and Levi wasn't irritated in the least. He picked the hoof back up and continued working on it. I took that opportunity to lure Annie over with gingersnaps and by the time Justy was done, Annie was standing nervously only pulling slightly on her lead. She ducked her backend away from Levi a few times but he was patient and kind and very steady.

"What's this from?" he asked, as he ran his hand over a long scar on Annie's back right leg. "Looks like a rope burn."

I explained about the junkyard. "I think she might have been tethered to something heavy that she dragged around—not only because of that scar, but when she runs, she looks behind her as if she thinks it might still be there."

He rubbed the scar. "Poor girl." Then he ran his fingers over a grayish patch on the front of the same leg. "This might be rain rot. Do you have any baby oil?" He stood up and patted her on the rear which made her skirt sideways for a second. "Hey, it's okay," he said to her. "I'm not going to hurt you." He looked at Mark and me. "She is skittish."

"Middleburg Humane brought her over a year ago Christmas eve. She was supposed to arrive the day before but it took them four hours to load her into the trailer and by that time it was dark so they just left her in overnight. It was freezing cold then, too."

I shook my head and shrugged. I don't second-guess their methods, having great admiration for the work they do under often extremely dire and very sad circumstances.

"They brought a draft mule, too—I had offered to take two horses for the winter, their choice."

Levi was slowly and carefully filing Annie's left back hoof, but he glanced up in appreciation to show he was listening.

I kept talking. "The equine manager led Bill the mule out of the trailer first and took him through the gate and I could hear Annie kicking the side of the trailer as if to say, 'Hey, what about me?'"

"After being in there all night I'm sure she wanted out," Mark interjected.

I nodded. "Anja led her off the trailer and through the gate, which I latched, and when Anja unhooked the lead, Annie took off for the farthest corner of the yard. Anja said her flight instinct was way off the charts."

Levi brightened up. "I know Anja. I've volunteered for them."

"Yeah," Mark said. "Anja's great. She's tiny but she led that gigantic mule like he was a puppy."

"I remember that mule," Levi said. "His feet were in terrible shape."

"That's why we couldn't keep him. They bought him at a livestock sale, they said the Amish had just used him up and by then he had white line disease. The foundation sent a farrier over here named Hank—do you know him? He was kind of surly."

Levi shook his head. "There are a lot of farriers around here. But there's also a lot of work, too, thankfully."

"Well," I continued. "Hank had to come every four weeks and Bill, the mule—we called him Bill after my father—he wasn't particularly fond of having that corrective shoe removed and replaced. The vet had to come to sedate him and they always discussed the dosage because he wasn't easy to work on but you don't want him to fall on you." We all laughed a little at that. "One time I was holding Bill while Hank worked to pry the shoe off and Bill started hopping away on three legs. 'Hold him, hold him!' Hank shouted as he hopped along with the mule's back leg wedged between his knees, and I tried, I did, but it was impossible. When a draft mule wants to go, there's nothing I could do about it."

"What was the vet doing?" Mark asked.

"Sitting on the fence. She and Hank were gossiping up a storm about some other farrier. So Hank and Bill are hopping and Hank's yelling at me to hold the mule still, and I'm trying with all my might, but it was like having the Empire State Building on a leash."

Levi liked that analogy. "Sounds like you could've used stocks like you use for cattle? Some animals are impossible unless they're confined—especially when they're in pain. They just want to get away from it."

"That's what Hank said the first time I met him. He even suggested that we build stocks. He said we could make money. I didn't even know what he was talking about but I looked up stocks online. They're like huge free-standing stalls and they cost a fortune. We were only keeping the mule for the winter. It's not as if we're a professional facility. We don't even have stall doors; why would we have stocks for shoeing! Our horses don't even wear shoes!"

Levi laughed. "So where is the mule now?"

"I think he's found a home in Lovettsville. But when Anja came to get him, she wasn't happy about the fact that she was going to have to go pick him up every month and take him to Aireshire Farm in Upperville because they're all set up for draft horses. I said, they're rich, maybe they'll adopt him. She said, they don't want him, but we're welcome to use their stocks."

"All the way from Marshall to Lovettsville to Upperville and back again?" Levi exclaimed. It was about twenty miles round trip on winding country roads, too.

"I know." Mark and I both shook our heads. The way the crow flies Marshall might not be so far from Lovettsville but when you have to use umpteen country roads it adds so much time.

"Lately with all the confiscated horses, Anja said she spends two days a week hauling horses," I added. "But she's amazing. Did you know she grew up in East

Germany before the Berlin wall came down? And she works two jobs. She's got so much determination, when she was trying to load Bill in the trailer he took off in the opposite direction and Anja kept up with him and got him turned around and brought him back. When she led him into the trailer, I said, 'I can't believe you did that.' I was thinking about the many times I had failed in my efforts to get Bill from point A to point B. She said, 'I just knew I wasn't going to let go.' I love that."

"That's great," Levi said. I was beginning to see he had a healthy dose of determination as well. Every time he reached toward Annie she would balk and he would persist. His manner was calm and kind. He'd speak to her in a soothing voice, stroke her neck for a bit, then cautiously lean down and ask for her hoof by squeezing gently on the tendon above the fetlock. She allowed him to trim and file each hoof, but she refused to let him place her front hoof on the hoof stand and after a few attempts, we all agreed it wasn't really necessary. I took her halter off and ran to open the gate to the big field. Mark and Levi and I watched as Danny, Justy and Annie tore through the gate and galloped across the field to the far side. I never tire of watching them run.

Ordinarily, I would be greatly relieved because it was almost over. But at that time we had two more horses, two recent rescues whose personalities I didn't know—Sunny and Zanzy—who were both haltered and obliviously munching hay in another yard. Sunny was a seven year-old palomino gelding, and Zanzy was a twenty-five year-old thoroughbred mare. Sunny was big and bossy, unruly and possibly dangerous, while Zanzy was emaciated and quite docile.

"I don't know if the palomino has ever had his feet done," I said worriedly. "The old mare used to be a racehorse so she obviously has, but the palomino won't lift up his feet for me."

"It should be all right," Levi said as he followed us into the next paddock.

"They've been with us just over a month," I told him.

He walked right up to Zanzy and stroked her shoulder. I attached the lead and he leaned over and ran his hand down over her knee. He gently squeezed her left fetlock and she lifted her hoof. Sunny tried to crowd around to see what was going on and Mark hooked him to a lead and walked him away a bit. He was very agitated and suddenly whinnied so loud I jumped. Levi didn't even look up from his work.

We talked about the snow that had been a constant since early December. "Mark's going crazy trying to keep us plowed. Everyone is." I reached my hand under Zanzy's blanket to make sure she was warm and dry. Sunny was blanketed, too. We had never needed to purchase expensive all-weather blankets for our horses because we had plenty of shelters and each one had a thick winter coat. But Sunny and Zanzy came from a place with little food and no shelter. I scratched Zanzy on the withers while Levi trimmed her first hoof.

"I'm from Wisconsin," he said. "I don't mind the snow."

Zanzy resisted lifting her back leg and he didn't force her, but gently and slowly encouraged her until it was just barely high enough for him to work on. "She probably has sore hocks. That's common in old horses. She might need a shot from the vet." He ran his hand over each leg before getting her to lift up her foot. She had scars on both front legs.

"One of those is a racing injury," I said, though he hadn't asked. "The other one came from kicking a hole in a lean-to. That's what they told me, the people who had them."

"You should have seen the place where we got them," Mark added. "No shelter, no grass, just weeds, and she lived there for twenty years."

Levi stood up and brushed off his apron. "They're lucky you took them."

"We couldn't leave them there," I said. Although I was already feeling overwhelmed with five horses, three on one side, two on the other, having to keep them separate, and I would feel even more so as winter set in with a vengeance. Though we had bought a ready-built run-in shed for the front pasture where Zanzy and Sunny were, they clung to the edge of the barn near where our other horses were, which was especially frustrating during the February blizzards. I'd see them hunched together skinny and cold against the onslaught and feel so frustrated, especially after we spent an entire afternoon digging a trench through the knee-deep snow so they could make their way back and forth. Still they huddled together at the corner of the fence while the beautiful three thousand dollar shelter stood brazenly empty.

    On that cold winter's day, Levi picked up his tools and approached Sunny in the corral. Mark held the big palomino steady with a tight grip on the lead. I stood nearby with Zanzy, Sunny's companion, hoping her presence would keep him calm. Sunny allowed Levi to pat him on the shoulder and run his hand down his leg but his hoof remained cemented to the ground. When Levi grasped it firmly and lifted, Sunny struggled fiercely, huge body heaving, as he yanked his leg again and again while Levi clung on. It certainly wasn't easy working on an obstinate eleven hundred-pound horse, one that was constantly trying to pull away. Levi was just as stubborn though and got the first hoof cleaned and filed evenly. After two false starts, he was able to hold the hoof still enough to trim the frog. But when he moved to Sunny's back left hoof, the big horse increased his resistance two-fold. Levi had to dodge and sidestep to avoid being kicked as he went over to the right front hoof, and although it took twice as long as it should have, he got that hoof done, too.

    Over the next quarter hour, Mark and Levi led the terrified horse from one flat spot to another on the frozen snow-covered ground, trying to find the magic place where he would calm down enough for Levi to work on his back hooves. But every time Levi took it in his grasp and began to file with the rasp, Sunny would hop backwards or veer sideways and yank his hoof out of

Levi's hold. Mark kept a firm grasp on Sunny's halter and I followed close by with Zanzy. My fingers and toes were completely frozen by that time and I was miserable. I began to wish Levi would just say he couldn't finish the palomino that day, even as I dreaded having to go through it again. But Levi persevered, seemingly impervious to the cold, and not daunted by the stubborn horse. After twenty minutes or so, I suggested that maybe we should get the vet to come with a tranquillizer. "Another time," I added hastily. I was freezing and just wanted to go inside!

Trying desperately to free himself from this seeming injustice, Sunny suddenly reared up, yanked his hoof out of Levi's hold, and sent him flying to land with a thud on the frozen ground. Mark swore as his arm was nearly yanked out of its socket, but he somehow managed to hold on.

Levi stood up amazingly still undaunted. "Do you have a chain?" he called to me.

I perked up; he wasn't going to quit. "I do. I'll run get it." I dropped Zanzy's lead, carefully skated over the icy ground, climbed the fence and hurried to the corncrib where we kept the halters and leads. Somewhere in there, and I dearly hoped I could find it fast, was an old red lead-line with a rusty chain attached. I had used it for my hound dog when she went swimming in the pond, because she would refuse to get out of the water and I'd have to haul her out like a giant fish. I rummaged around frantically until I found it in a cardboard box under the table. When I returned, Levi deftly hooked the chain end to Sunny's halter, ran the chain over his gums, and handed the end of the lead to Mark. Both back hooves were trimmed as Sunny squirmed and made ridiculous faces, but with the chain on his gums, he did not try to get away. Horses' mouths are just that sensitive, Sunny didn't move for fear of pain.

...

A few weeks later, in February of 2010, we were about to get our second major snowfall of the season. Levi stopped in one afternoon to see if he could buy more hay. He knew we had sold out of round bales but that we had a barn full of square bales. "My horses haven't eaten today," he told me.

Mark was at work and the road to the back barn was already covered with new-fallen snow. "I don't think you should try going up the ramp even if you have four-wheel drive," I said. "But if you park down below you can have what you can carry." I noticed he was driving a different truck, a shiny black Dodge, much newer than the Ford he'd brought before. This one had heavy-duty tires and a carriage company insignia on the driver's door.

I had just finished mucking the front horse barn, when he drove up from the barn about ten minutes later, and I saw that the back of his pick-up was stacked to the cab roof-line with hay bales. He turned off the motor, got out, came to the fence and reported that he had ten. "I don't have my checkbook; can I stop by later with a check?"

"Sure," I said. Then I asked him, "Do you work for a carriage company?"

"I own a carriage company," he said proudly. "Or I will in a year if things go right and I get it paid off." I was beginning to understand that Levi was very open about himself. He described his two beautiful carriages pulled by either his percherons, or his haflingers. "And when I drive, I wear a tuxedo, top hat and white driving gloves."

He reminded me of a happy kid with a look-what-I-can-do bravado. I made some pleasant remark and asked if he did weddings.

"We do lots of weddings, parades, anniversary parties, birthday parties. I'm doing a four year-old's birthday party in April, over in Potomac, Maryland. The grandfather has a very well-known name, Marriott. They've hired the Cinderella package which means I'll be putting sparkles on my haflingers' hooves."

"Well, if anyone can paint their hooves with sparkles, you can!" We laughed and he got back into his truck. I waved him off, and marveled at his energy. He had just moved ten bales of hay out of the barn down the long snow covered barn ramp and into his truck in about ten minutes.

The snow never stopped that day or the next. Not only were schools and local governments closed, but the Federal government shut down, as well. Mark plowed our long driveway for hours back and forth, and would come inside from time to time to complain that there was nowhere to dump the snow. "There's a canyon out there now. The driveway's a canyon."

The wind never died down either, and six-foot drifts collected around him like ocean swells. Everyone was snowbound, even our neighbor, Eddie, who had pulled an enormous snow-blower behind his tractor during the previous snowstorm and heroically plowed us out like a great savior. But when Mark called him after six hours straight of plowing in vain, Eddie said he had the same problem at his place, impenetrable snow drifts all along his drive ten-feet deep; and Eddie's drive is about four times as long as ours. We had all grown weary of declaring: This isn't supposed to happen here. We aren't supposed to get this much snow.

During that week, Levi called several times saying he needed more hay. Mark told him the first time he called that we couldn't get to the barn. The next time he called he asked if we were plowed out yet. Mark said, "I can't even plow my way out to the road. I haven't even tried getting to the barn. You're going to have to find another place to get hay, Levi." The only other place to get hay was Southern States and the price per bale was through the roof. Levi called us the next day and the next, asking if Mark had managed to get out to the hay barn yet. The answer was still no.

One afternoon Mark and I were both out shoveling trenches for the horses to get from the barn to the water trough and round bale rack. We were wearing our heavy winter coveralls that were already hard enough to maneuver around in, but with the snow thigh-high, we kept losing our balance and landing on our butts like a couple of clowns. Suddenly a figure appeared at the end of the driveway and we watched as he made his way toward us holding a snow shovel. It was Levi. He had left his truck back on the road and walked up, he said, to help dig a track to the big barn.

We both stared at him, incredulous, and Mark exclaimed: "Levi, how can we dig out a path with a shovel when I can't even do it with the loader? It's almost a half mile to the barn."

"There's some old hay in this loft," I said, motioning behind me toward the horse barn. "Our horses like it. I think it's like aged bourbon or something. We don't actually feed it to them but sometimes if I need to lure them out of the barn I'll throw a few down and they gobble it up."

"Could I have some of that?" He looked to Mark.

"Okay. Sure. You want to bring your truck over? I'll try to make you a track." Mark got on the tractor and began making runs down toward the road, scooping up buckets full of snow, heaping it onto the tall piles on the edge of the field, over and over again. I showed Levi how to get up into the loft. He climbed up and said, "This looks okay. This looks pretty good." He threw down five or six bales and stacked them by the fence.

I leaned against my snow shovel. "Mark says you live on Ashby Farm Circle?"

He nodded and pointed into the snowy expanse toward the big barn. "You can almost see my house from here. It's just on the other side of the field."

"Is it the brick one right in the curve of the road with a gazebo?" I knew it had to be but I wasn't about to admit that I'd been spying.

"That's it. There's a pond, a center aisle barn and a riding arena, too. I'm leasing it. I know the owner."

"Do you have family?"

"No, just me."

Mark came back and parked the tractor. "Best I can do. But you should be able to get up this far with your four-wheel drive."

Levi thanked us and went to get his truck, drove back, loaded the hay, and he was off. I told Mark about how he lived alone in that big fancy house. We both thought it was odd. It just wasn't the kind of house we would imagine he'd live in.

Winter finally ended; spring made a brief appearance, and then it was summer. We used to have real springs in Virginia but for the past few years the temperature goes from seventy to ninety in a week and stays there. The hay was cut and baled and Levi came to do trims on the horses and we chit-chatted while he worked. The carriage business was slow in mid-summer, but he kept busy shoeing horses. He mentioned that his two boys were coming to visit. "I hope they'll like it here. I thought we'd go fishing and I'm trying to think of some other things to do with them."

I was shocked. "You have sons?" This is the kind of thing I usually find out about people fairly quickly; especially talkative people like Levi. Yet I had known him for six months and I'd never before heard mention of children.

"Yes, Samuel is eleven and Jacob is seven. They live in Wisconsin. I'm divorced from their mother." He was uncharacteristically reticent and sad.

I changed the subject and told him how much easier it was now that the palomino was gone. "We traded him to this really cute girl in Maryland. She's going to train Annie in exchange. Of course I'm already freaking out about getting Annie in the trailer." Annie heard her name. She was grazing nearby with one ear cocked.

"Oh, she'll go in," he said assuredly.

He was finished with Danny I led the big red horse away and released him. When I brought Zanzy over he hardly recognized her. "Is this the same horse?"

"Yep. She's gained about two hundred pounds, and she's a lot spunkier, too." As if to prove it, Zanzy gave him a hard time, refusing to pick up her back feet, playing tug-o-war with her hind leg.

When he was finished we made a date for the fall and I wished him well. "Have fun with your boys," I said. He agreed that he would, and looked happy at the prospect. I paid him by check since bartering season hadn't begun yet and as I watched him drive away I thought about how much easier the whole farrier process was with him. Before, it was hard to get a farrier on the phone, scheduling was difficult, and they were usually late. If the horses acted up – even playfully, the farrier could be annoyed, some were harsh. Levi either answers the phone right away (I have since noticed he drives with a Bluetooth in his ear), or he calls back the same day. He schedules right then and there. He is usually on time (or he calls if he's tied up at a previous appointment), and he is very competent with the horses. Plus he is just pleasant to be around.

...

One sunny crisp afternoon in late September 2010, Levi came to do hoof trims, and while he worked, we got to talking. As these conversations go, we started out with the weather. The trees on the Blue Ridge Mountains behind our Virginia farmhouse were beginning to turn orange-red and I said I was going to miss summer. "Although I like fall, now, too, since I don't have to go to school anymore."

"Oh, were you a teacher?" he asked.

"No, I was thinking about when I was kid. Fall meant going back to school. I never liked school much."

"I didn't either," he said. "I only went through the eighth grade."

I was shocked. I looked at him, and being a mother, my immediate reaction was: "What did your parents think about that?"

"Oh, that's what they wanted," he replied. "I grew up Amish in Wisconsin."

I stood there with my mouth hanging open. It explained so much about him; his patience, his steady demeanor, his politeness, his competence with the horses, his perseverance, and his work ethic— thinking we'd use a hand shovel in deep snow to dig out the half-mile road to the hay barn!

"Do you still see your family?" I asked. It was my round-about way of trying to discern if he was still Amish —which I seriously doubted for many reasons—the Bluetooth in his ear, his buzz-cut hair, his store-bought blue jeans and the Aussie Down Under tee shirt.

"No. Not since I left."

I was trying to pace myself. There was so much I wanted to know but I couldn't bombard him with questions that would just be rude. I remembered my long-ago comment about how the Amish had just used up Bill the mule and my face reddened. He hadn't said anything. Maybe he hadn't heard. I hoped not.

When he finished with Danny, I took off his halter and let him go. Then I clipped the lead on Justy's halter.

"Are you estranged from your family?" I asked. "Mark has a brother who hasn't spoken to anyone in the family in years. He didn't go to his mother's deathbed and he didn't attend her funeral even though he got phone calls from three or four family members."

He began to rasp Justy's left front hoof. "No, I'm not estranged, but I might as well be. They don't want to see me."

I didn't know much about the Amish, but I did recall something about shunning probably from a "Law and Order" episode. "Is it the Amish who shun those who leave?" I asked.

"Yes." He brought out the hoof stand and placed Justy's hoof on it. Then he abruptly stood up and declared, "The things that have happened to me you wouldn't believe. People are always telling me my life would make a great movie. Did you see the movie, Witness? That's how I grew up."

Justy didn't miss his chance to remove his foot from the hoof stand and he seemed to sense we weren't even paying attention to him, so he began to butt me in the chest with his head. I told him to stop it. Levi stepped up, took Justy's halter firmly and told him to settle down.

Justy dropped his head and I stroked his neck. "He's a lot happier now that Sunny's gone," I commented. "Do you remember the wound you discovered on his leg last spring? It turned out to be a broken bone. That little one inside the cannon bone that isn't really important but it still caused him a lot of pain. Sunny kicked him. They were both vying to be second in command."

"Oh, yes." Levi stood up and studied Justy's leg. Then he patted his neck. "Poor guy. Don't you know Danny's the boss?"

I told Levi that Sunny's new owner had put shoes on him and gotten his teeth floated. "He's turning into a real gentleman."

"That's great." He finished with Justy and I clipped the lead on Annie's halter. Then I let Justy go. Annie was shy but very cooperative. Zanzy was last and she put up the most resistance.

"She's a lot more mischievous now that she's put on weight and has energy." I said. "I think the people who had them before were feeding them out of the same bucket! Naturally Sunny was getting everything."

He shook his head. "That's crazy." After awhile he asked in his characteristic old-fashioned way, "Do you work outside the home?"

"I'm a writer," I replied.

He looked up excitedly. "You mean you could write my story?"

I was surprised by his innocent enthusiasm. I was also caught off-guard. Agreeing to write someone's story isn't something to venture into without a great deal of thought. I had learned this the hard way, having gotten myself involved in a few projects that were all work and no pay.

"Well, I could," I said tentatively. I still wasn't accustomed to his naiveté. But after I heard some of his stories, especially the one about faking his death, we decided to give it a try. We commenced meeting every month or so and he'd talk while I took notes and asked questions and he commented once, "It's like you're my therapist!" For I did have to probe quite a bit, not for dates and details, Levi was encyclopedic about those, but for the real reason he left which of course had a lot to do with freedom and modern conveniences but essentially boiled down to his independent ideology.

I was enthralled with his descriptions of a lifestyle I found to be right out of the 19th century. When I learned that he grew up without electricity for instance my first comment was, "What? No hot showers?"

"Yes, the first time I had a hot shower I didn't want to get out. We never brushed our teeth, either," he added, and my eyebrows went up. "Oh," he said, "I went to the dentist when I left the Amish and my teeth were okay. I also used to wear glasses but last year I had laser surgery." He told me he had been nearsighted most of his youth, but his parents didn't even get him glasses until he was seventeen. "I couldn't believe how much I missed seeing in life!"

At one of our interview sessions, after we got started on the book idea, I told Levi about the author who went on "Oprah" to talk about his memoir and how it became a big scandal when it was discovered that he had made up his story. Levi's remark was, "Do you think we should go on Oprah with our book? Would that help get it some attention?"

By that time I was accustomed to his lack of knowledge about pop culture and I knew his question was completely earnest so I gave him a straight forward answer, although I couldn't help laughing just a bit. "Of course it would help but getting on Oprah is almost impossible." [Her show was still on the air in 2010].

I had previously tried to explain to him that getting published was almost impossible, too. But Levi is admittedly and proudly optimistic. It's a good measure of how insulated his life was from the time he was born in 1974 until he left the Amish in 1996, and the many, many obstacles he overcame to get where he is today.

Every time I came home from one of our interview sessions I'd tell Mark what I had learned that day and his reaction was always the same. "This is going to be big. Those stories are incredible!"

And Levi's story is incredible, especially to those of us who grew up in these modern times, those of us who had so many advantages not to mention all of the conveniences that go way beyond the basics of electricity and indoor plumbing.

Let it be said, too, that Levi grew up in an Old Order Amish settlement. His grandfather was a bishop, his father was a minister, they had no modern conveniences, they were very inclusive, and they desired little interaction or exposure to the outside world. They did not have Rumspringa, which is when some Amish communities allow or even encourage their young people to go out and experience the world before committing to the church.

In Levi's Amish community to leave the Amish was to go with the devil and to be recognized no more. As Levi says of his sister, "I'm dead to her now. I don't exist."

In Levi's point of view this is what being Amish was like; this story only references the old world order in which he lived. So, for example, when he says, Amish don't have telephones, or Amish don't drive, he is talking about the way it was for him, in that world, which was the only world he knew until he set up his escape to look like a stabbing and a kidnapping. He was that desperate and the situation was that dire. If they didn't think he'd been taken against his will, and if they didn't believe him to be dead, they would come after him and beseech him endlessly to return to the Amish. Their methods were mentally tortuous and he knew he wouldn't be able to withstand what he calls their brainwashing.

When Levi talks about his early years he says, "Always in the back of my mind I knew that I was going to leave but you'd get a sharp stick reprimand if you said a word, because that was the devil talking to you." So he kept his feelings to himself and bided his time.

"When I was growing up, my 2nd cousin and his wife had a lot of trouble with the church. They left the Amish and then they divorced. You don't talk to those people at the grocery store." He shook his head at the memory, having since been divorced himself, and more than once he has been turned away from his parents' door by his father, his mother not even able to step into view and say hello to him or meet her grandsons.

"I remember shortly before I left," he continues. "I was at a funeral for Sam Gingerich, and his nephew Joe was there. My dad and Joe used to be friends. Joe was no longer Amish and he wore a cowboy suit. He was dressed to the nines. We just stared and I felt amazed by the sight of him and in awe that he would come before us looking like that."

Levi saw his brother, Samuel, at his grandfather's funeral in 2005. "He only answered my questions. He wouldn't look me in the eye. People thought if anyone in the family was going to leave the Amish it would have been Samuel, but he would never leave, he is too dependent upon the church community. He's also a natural born hypocrite, smoking behind the barn, even drinking alcohol from time to time. And he refuses to meet my eyes now that I'm no longer Amish."

Levi isn't sorry that he left. He concludes: "It feels like my whole life back then I was secretly fascinated about leaving. I always wanted to drive a truck. I own two trucks now. I enjoy this lifestyle. The main thing I miss about not being Amish is my family."

Levi has many nieces and nephews whom he does not know. Almost fifteen years after he left the Amish and four years after he divorced Rosanna and moved across the country, one of his sisters wrote him a letter that said:

You should go back to your family and come back to the Amish and then I can tell my children about you.

"I'm worse than dead to her unless I do," Levi says. "I don't exist. Her children, if they think about it, may wonder about the gap between my older sister and my younger sister but no one will tell them, Oh yes, you had an uncle Levi but he left the Amish." Levi said he wanted his story told so that his sons would know about his past and their heritage.

Photographs

This is Levi in 2012. Notice his non-Amish buzz-cut and the Bluetooth in his ear.

Levi dons his Amish hat. Also decidedly non-Amish are the wristwatch, Aussie T-shirt and shorts.

Levi's parents' house in the foreground is where he grew up. The house in back is where Levi lived with his wife—where he left the blood trail when he faked his abduction. One day after they left the Amish, when they knew everyone would be at church, Levi and his wife drove to his parents' farm and took this photo.

Levi driving Thunder and Lightning, his original percherons bought at auction shortly after he left the Amish.

Levi driving the Cinderella carriage pulled by his haflingers, Doc and Dan. The draft ponies have plumes in their manes and sparkles on their hooves.

Levi works on my retired racehorse Zanzy.

Round bales of orchard grass hay.

References and Resources

I've done quite a bit of research on the Amish and three books have been especially informative and inspiring: John Hostetler's <u>Amish Society</u>, Raymond Bial's <u>Visit to Amish Country</u>, and Sue Bender's <u>Plain and Simple.</u>

The Philadelphia Inquirer calls <u>Amish Society</u>, "the definitive book on one of America's most misunderstood communities." I have the 4th edition which has been updated, 435 pages of meticulous research, an extensive bibliography, maps, charts and even black and white photographs of Amish children running into the cornfield to escape the public school bus; eighth graders doing their sums on the one-room schoolhouse blackboard; an open top buggy full of young folks flirting and laughing; Amish men waiting to testify before Congress for exemption from welfare benefits; and young women in bonnets and long dresses sitting hip-to-hip on a bench before an immense barn under construction, its rafters open to the sky and swarming with Amish men.

Hostetler, who left the Amish to pursue higher education, is emeritus professor of anthropology and sociology and former director of the Center for Anabaptist and Pietist Studies at Elizabethtown College. The center's website is the best source for factual information on the Internet, and was a great help in writing this book.
<u>http://www2.etown.edu/amishstudies</u>.

Note: The Amish wedding vows I wrote on page 33 came from <u>Amish Society</u> as does the description of an Amish funeral on page 88 and details about wedding supper match-ups, marriage permissions and announcement customs on page 104.

Raymond Bial's <u>Visit to Amish Country</u> has over a hundred color photographs of Amish buildings, animals and objects (not people, though, since they do not want to be photographed), and includes instructive essays and descriptive captions, with good lyrical writing. Bial celebrates the beauty of all things Amish.

Sue Bender's <u>Plain and Simple</u>, is a carefully written memoir of her longing to be like the Amish. She stayed with two Amish families back in the 1980s and concluded: "For so long I needed to see the Amish with romantic eyes. But they aren't perfect." The book includes charming black and white illustrations by Bender and her husband.

Hostetler, John A. <u>Amish Society.</u> 4th ed. Baltimore: Johns Hopkins University Press, 1993. The classic text on Amish life which focuses on three large settlements: Holmes County, Ohio; Lancaster County, Pa.; and the Elkhart-LaGrange settlement in Northern Indiana. [Much of the field work was done in the 1960s and 70s but many of the interpretations of Amish culture are enduring.] [Amish Studies website.]

Igou, Brad, comp. *The Amish in Their Own Words. Scottdale, PA: Herald Press,1999. [Selections of Amish writings from the Amish magazine Family Life.] [Amish Studies website.]

Kraybill, Donald B. Concise Encyclopedia of Amish, Brethren, Hutterites, and Mennonites. Baltimore: Johns Hopkins University Press, 2010. [340 entries providing a succinct overview of the history, religious beliefs, and cultural practices of the more than 200 different Anabaptist groups in North America.] [Amish Studies website.]

Kraybill, Donald B. The Riddle of Amish Culture. 2nd ed. Baltimore: Johns Hopkins University Press, 2001. [A socio-cultural history of the Lancaster Amish settlement with interpretations that apply to other settlements. Shows how the Amish negotiate socio-cultural change in the context of modern society.] [Amish Studies website.]

Nolt, Steven M., and Thomas J. Meyers. Plain Diversity: Amish Cultures and Identities. Baltimore: Johns Hopkins University Press, 2007. [A cultural-historical study of diverse Amish groups in Indiana. Offers a conceptual framework for understanding Amish diversity.] [Amish Studies website.]

Hyperlinks

Amish Studies website. Young Center for Anabaptist and Pietist Studies, Elizabethtown College. http://www2.etown.edu/amishstudies.

Amish 101
http://www.oacountry.com/amishknowlegebase1
http://www.ohiosamishcountry.com Amish 101
http://www.amish.net "America's first website devoted to Amish Country information, Amish made products and tourism services."
http://amishamerica.com a web blog
http://www.thebudgetnewspaper.com Amish newspaper
http://www.jsonline.com/news/wisconsin/29483974.html July 14, 2008 Milwaukee News Sentinel Article about Amish clashes with Government in Wisconsin
BBC website Amish site: http://www.bbc.co.uk/religion/religions/christianity/subdivisions/amish_1.shtml

Acknowledgments

I am grateful to Levi Hochstetler for sharing his story and trusting me to write it. About midway through the writing of the book I realized it couldn't be straight non-fiction as there were just too many details I had to fill in. Plus there was the major absence of his ex-wife's point of view. So we agreed that I would write it as a novel based on a true story and that is what it is.

Proper names and identifying details have been changed throughout the book but everything about Levi really did happen. The only part that is fictional is Rosanna's and that was fun for me because her life, as I imagined it, was so vastly different from mine.

I am particularly indebted to my daughter Erin Pfoutz for editing the original manuscript, and to my daughter Nicki Pfoutz for suggesting creative writing enhancements. Much gratitude goes out to my husband Mark for his encouragement, and to my friends June Krupsaw and Linda Carlson for reading the manuscript. Also thanks to June Krupsaw for her photographic expertise.

Photographs of Levi and his carriages are courtesy of the Shenandoah Carriage Company website.

Many thanks to my daughter Erin Pfoutz for locating the actual article about Levi's faked abduction in the August 27, 1996 Milwaukee Journal Sentinel. Permission to reprint was granted by NewsBank NewsLibrary.

The End

Made in the USA
Las Vegas, NV
14 June 2021